BLOOD
IS A SPECIAL JUICE

By

JACK SPENSER, M.D.

CONTENTS

PROLOGUE

March 1973

It was my night to admit patients. I went to the ward to do a history and physical on a seventeen-year-old male patient who had come to the emergency room with a bad episode of coughing up blood and shortness of breath. The ER stabilized him and sent him to the internal medicine floor to be admitted. His name was Tom Eatherly.

I was surprised that a seventeen-year-old was sent to the internal medicine ward instead of pediatrics, but when I entered the patient's room, I saw why: he was six feet tall, a little too big for a pediatric bed. He was cachectic. I looked at his chart; he weighed 130 pounds.

Tom was sitting up in his bed, breathing through an oxygen mask. I introduced myself to him and his mother, who was sitting on the other side of the bed. I took the remaining chair and sat down across from her. As I read the patient's thick medical chart, he looked at me calmly, even though he was obviously out of breath, breathing at twice the normal respiratory rate. According to the chart, he had been like this since he was five years old, when he was diagnosed with idiopathic pulmonary hemosiderosis, which is jargon for saying he was bleeding into his lungs for unknown reasons. Over the years this bleeding had caused a lot of lung damage, mainly scarring.

"I guess after twenty admissions to the hospital, you're used to this," I said.

He shrugged.

I continued to read the chart, which I can briefly summarize: the disease had just about killed him. There wasn't much more to learn from the medical history, so I stopped reading and proceeded to do a physical exam.

1

Beads of sweat moistened the skin above his upper lip. He was working hard just to breathe while sitting in his bed. No wonder he was thin. He had no spare energy to use to put on muscle or fat. I listened to the back of his chest with my stethoscope, first right side, then left side. He was breathing rapidly, and I listened to his lungs working hard. The breath coming in was a whoosh coming toward me like the wind in a cave; breath out, and the wind retreated. I put the bell of my stethoscope on the front of his chest and listened to his heart beat rapidly, like two bongo drums, one struck immediately after the other – the rhythm of a frantic war dance.

I took another look at his medical chart. His previous twenty admissions had been like the present admission – rapid breathing and rapid heart rate – a recurrent struggle to stay alive. It took a great respiratory effort simply to get oxygen to what little tissue he had.

The patient's mom went to the hospital cafeteria to get some supper. I hoped she would survive. The food there was terrible.

I wrote up my history and physical findings and put them in the chart. It didn't take long. The diagnosis and findings were obvious, just a continuation of the malady he'd suffered from for most of his life.

Tom turned on the TV. It was Monday, late March, and the final game of the NCAA basketball tournament was about to start – Memphis State versus UCLA.

"You mind if I stay and watch?" I asked.

He shrugged.

I pulled the chair around to where I could see the TV and not block his view. It wasn't much of a game. It was obvious early on that UCLA would win easily. Bill Walton, who played for UCLA, was unstoppable, scoring at will. He was the best college basketball player I ever saw. My mind wandered. *This is my rebellion*, I thought, watching and thinking about a basketball game instead of studying, what I was supposed to do. I was well into my third year of medical school, and I was goofing off. Oh, I was taking care of my patients alright, or at least I thought I was, but I wasn't studying the way I was supposed to. Instead I'd become a dreamer, a writer, an artist. In med school that mindset will get you flunked out. If I didn't start bookin' it, I wouldn't make it to graduation. Hell, I wouldn't make it through the year.

Until then I'd lived a studious, disciplined life – had to. My college premed courses had been tough, at least for me, and the competition to get into medical school was brutal. There were seventy-five freshman premed students in my college class, but only seven made it to med school. To be one of them, I had to be focused and ruthless. While my classmates were joining fraternities, partying, marching for peace, and getting laid – I studied my butt off.

My hard work paid off. I was admitted to the medical school of Ivory University in Nashville, Tennessee. The university was nicknamed the "Harvard of the South," but truth be told, medical school was more of a trade school rather than a university. Learning to be a doctor is like learning to be an airline pilot or a car mechanic. Mastering a large body of knowledge and learning some skills were the tasks at hand, not anything to do with creativity.

The first two years of med school covered the "basic sciences" – anatomy, biochemistry, physiology, neuroanatomy, pathology, microbiology, pharmacology…important subjects to be sure, and actually reasonably interesting, but *not* designed to nourish the soul or discern a philosophy of life. The soul could take care of itself. To the faculty and students it was obvious that the best use of a life was to be the best physician you could possibly be. To be a doctor was a calling, not a job, and for the most part I was okay with that. But oh how I yearned for an English course, philosophy course, religion course – anything to break up the monotony of scientific medicine – a course that would let me think, create, and breathe. However, that was not to be. I felt like a programmed robot.

The third year was a little bit better because we encountered real live patients instead of cadavers, test tubes, and microscopes. Still, the emphasis was on assimilating a huge body of medical knowledge and learning skills – how to use a stethoscope, draw blood, do a lumbar puncture, insert a nasogastric tube…new tasks to learn every day. There was little time for anything else.

I was midway through a ten-week rotation in internal medicine, which had followed rotations in pediatrics, obstetrics, psychiatry, orthopedics, and neurology. When I finished with internal medicine, I would have a ten-week rotation in surgery. Then I would have a week of written final exams.

Ah! Final exams! That's what I was worried about. I wasn't ready for them because I wasn't studying the way I was supposed to. Instead I was writing stories, using the much-neglected creative part of my brain. My rational brain was plumb wore out.

At the end of the first half it was time to get my scut work done. I drew some blood from Tom, started an IV, and collected a urine sample. I took my leave from this unfortunate patient. I carried the blood and urine samples to the small lab down the hall and did some tests. I was by myself. I checked to see if my patient was anemic, which would make his condition worse, and I checked his white blood cell count to make sure he didn't have evidence of inflammation or infection, which was about the last thing he needed. I made a peripheral blood smear, stained it, and looked at it through the microscope. Finally I did a urinalysis.

Everything checked out okay. My patient didn't have anemia or an infection or anything else to complicate his illness – the problems causing his admission to the hospital were apparently just an exacerbation of his idiopathic pulmonary hemosiderosis. That was bad enough.

It was 9 p.m. Since I was on call, going home was not an option. What I needed to do was go to the library and read up on idiopathic pulmonary hemosiderosis so I would be conversant about this patient's rare disease when I presented him at rounds the next morning. But I didn't do that.

Instead I went to the sleeping quarters, which were just down the hall from the nursing station. The two beds in the room were separated by a nightstand with a lamp and telephone on top. One bed was for me, and the other was for the internal medicine intern who was on call with me. Both of us would be spending the night in the hospital, although typically if you were on call, you were working or studying rather than sleeping. My work was done for the moment, and I didn't feel like studying. I took off my shoes, pulled out Michael Crichton's book *The Andromeda Strain* from a drawer in the nightstand, and settled in the bed to read it. A couple of years earlier this book had been made into a movie, which I didn't get to see. Michael Crichton was a hero to me – a physician and a writer. I wanted to "be like Mike."

I had just started reading when Felix Weinberg, a hematology fellow, came into the room, looking for the intern. He was a short thin man with wire-frame glasses, who always looked nervous. He was looking for the intern because he needed to discuss a patient with him. Seeing only me, Felix picked up the phone and paged the intern. Then we waited. Dr. Weinberg noticed the book I was reading.

"I went to med school with that guy," he said.

"Michael Crichton?"

"Yeah. He was in my class at Harvard."

"Wow. What was he like?"

"Different."

"How?"

"Well, for one thing he was really *tall*, like almost seven feet."

"But what was he like, his personality?"

"He was a quiet guy. We all thought he was kind of crazy. The rest of us were all driven to become good doctors, with all kinds of peer pressure, same as here – to work hard, study hard. Medicine was an obsession. I mean, medical school was its own world, like the outside world didn't even exist."

"Same as here."

"Yeah. But Michael Crichton didn't buy into all that. His interest in medicine would come and go. He wasn't very popular...until *The Andromeda Strain* was published and became a bestseller. Then everyone wanted to be his friend. He lives in LA now, never did practice medicine, didn't even do an internship. I'm not sure what he's doing now."

"Is he happy?"

"If I had his money, I'd be happy."

"I'd like to write," I said. "But I doubt if I have his talent."

"Stick to medicine. Look, Michael Crichton was never supposed to be a doctor. He didn't want to make the effort."

"Yeah, the effort. I'm struggling."

"It's normal to struggle in med school from time to time, especially third year; it happens to all of us."

"I dunno."

"Okay. But don't do something stupid like quitting. I did that one time, during my internship. I'd been up all night as usual, and that morning I was overwhelmed with stuff I had to do. I just couldn't go on. I wrote a letter of resignation and handed it in to whoever was in the Medicine

Department Office and went home. By that afternoon I was so bored I returned to the hospital and went back to work. Nobody said anything."

The intern, Jeff Scott, walked into the room. He was a blond athletic guy. During his undergraduate years, he played basketball at Oklahoma State, where he had been coached by the legendary Hank Iba.

Jeff said, "You paged me?"

Felix said, "Yeah, I did. I want to talk to you about that twenty-three-year-old man, the patient with gallstones, the one who had a cholecystectomy?"

"John Rogers?"

"Right. That's the one. I want to do a bone marrow exam on him."

"Okay. Why?"

"Twenty-three is awfully young to have your gallbladder out."

"Right."

"And he has three siblings, and they've all had their gallbladders out at young ages."

"Right."

"So I'm wondering whether he has something hereditary, like hereditary spherocytosis. I looked at his peripheral blood smear, and that fits, and I think there's a good chance that's what he has."

John turned to me, not wanting to miss a chance to quiz me and maybe teach me something. He asked, "What does the peripheral blood smear look like in hereditary spherocytosis?"

I answered, "The red blood cells look like spheres instead of biconcave discs. Also they look smaller than normal – microspherocytes."

"How is that related to this patient needing his gallbladder out?" asked John.

"His red blood cells are misshapen, so they get destroyed in the spleen and elsewhere. The hemolysis releases hemoglobin into the blood. The hemoglobin in turn is metabolized by macrophages into bilirubin, which goes to the liver, which sends the bilirubin to the biliary system, which includes the gallbladder. All that excess bilirubin clogs up the gallbladder, which leads to gallstones – and a cholecystectomy."

"Right," said Felix. "What will the bone marrow show?"

"Production of a lot of red blood cells, excessive erythropoiesis, to replace the spherical red blood cells, which are defective and destroyed and don't live very long. His red blood cell production will be revved up so he doesn't get anemic."

"Correct," said Jeff.

"Why not do an osmotic fragility test instead of a bone marrow exam?" I asked.

Felix and Jeff looked at me, then looked around and didn't say anything. Finally Felix said, "The bone marrow procedure is scheduled for 10 a.m. tomorrow, after rounds." Felix left.

Jeff said to me, "I don't have an answer for you about why a bone marrow exam instead of an osmotic fragility test."

"The osmotic fragility test would be a heck of a lot easier."

"Yeah, but the bone marrow procedure is already scheduled. Dr. Weinberg wants the patient to have a bone marrow, the patient has signed a permit to have a bone marrow, the nurses have scheduled the bone marrow, the bone marrow kit has been ordered to the bedside, and the patient's family thinks he's having a bone marrow…too late to undo all that. Mr. Rogers is gonna have a bone marrow exam whether he needs one or not."

Uncharacteristically the rest of the night was quiet, and I got some sleep. I dreamed I was walking down a flight of stairs with other members of my class, and we were headed to the library to study. Suddenly I vaulted over the bannister, and I was wedged between the stairs and a wall – hanging there, suspended in space. Finally I felt my feet touch the floor. I looked around, and I was alone. I walked along a hallway and then turned a corner and came to a door on my right. I looked in. My classmates were in a circle, crouched around Felix Weinberg and Jeff Scott, and they were reciting information about hereditary spherocytosis in a monotone, like they were at church reciting the Apostles' Creed. In my dream I say to myself pathetically, "This is my rebellion. All I can do is throw myself at the mercy of the school and offer to repeat my third year."

I woke up at 5:30 a.m. and wrote words on a yellow legal pad, the first draft of a story about a young lad with idiopathic pulmonary hemosiderosis, and about a young man who was going to have a bone marrow exam for no good reason, and how I felt like a postulant in a monastery.

The words came out like bubbles from a champagne bottle that has been shaken up and then uncorked, spilling onto the paper.

I tried to discern what my dream meant. Joseph interpreted dreams for pharaoh, and that worked out pretty well for him. But I wasn't Joseph.

And I wasn't prepared for rounds, but it was too late to do anything about that. I made myself presentable, grabbed a quick breakfast, hoping to survive one more day of hospital food, and hurried off to morning rounds, which started punctually at 7 a.m.

Rounds were bedside visits by an entourage of students, house staff and an "attending" physician (i.e., faculty member), who led the group through the medical ward, stopping at each room and bedside along the way. In theory, the purpose of rounds was to check on the patients, assess how they were doing, and make plans for what to do next; this was an ideal setting for Socratic-type teaching with the attending as Socrates, and the rest of us as his followers. In practice, however, rounds seemed to me to be something different. Because most of the diseases on the internal medicine ward were treatable, but incurable – diabetes, hypertension, congestive heart failure, cancer…my perception of rounds was a bunch of people standing around talking about their dying patients.

I was dressed in khaki pants, a light blue short-sleeved shirt, and a dark blue tie; my short white coat indicated that I was a medical student. The interns and residents were similarly dressed except they had white pants in addition to the short white coat. The attending replaced the white pants and short white coat with a long white coat over street attire; of course he had on a tie. The few females in the group were attired in a similar fashion with dresses and blouses replacing the pants and shirts, but still with the white coats with lengths corresponding to seniority. Uniform and rank were important. There were twelve of us. The overall appearance of the group was that of a large white hen followed by a disorganized group of chicks.

We moved languidly from room to room, patient to patient. At each patient's bedside the chief resident would act as compere by telling the attending the patient's name and relating a very brief explanation of why the patient was in the hospital. Then the student would take over and present the pertinent information about the patient to the attending, with members of the house staff pitching in as needed.

Everything went fine until we got to my patient, Tom Eatherly, who had idiopathic pulmonary hemosiderosis. My job, as a student, was to do two things:

1. Present the patient's history and physical exam findings.
2. Discuss the disease the patient suffered from – etiology, pathophysiology, treatment, prognosis, and the like.

I did okay with item number one. I struck out on item number two because I hadn't done any studying, and it showed.

The attending, Dr. Hartmann, a tall Teutonic-appearing distinguished gentleman, asked, "What is the etiology of this disease?"

I answered, "Since 'idiopathic' is in the name, I assume no one knows." I knew that what I said wasn't all that clever, but it was all I had. No one was amused.

"That's quite an assumption, don't you think? For example, when the disease was first described, 'idiopathic,' or unknown, may have been an appropriate term, shorthand, a placeholder if you will. That doesn't mean we have to stay in ignorance."

"I'm still in ignorance."

"You sure are. Does anyone here have a clue about this disease? Miss Murtaugh?"

Diane Murtaugh was from South Carolina and went to college at Emory. She had light brown hair, an excellent figure, and beautiful legs, which she showed off with tastefully short dresses. She was a good friend of mine, a platonic friend, by her choice, not mine.

She said, "The theory is that there is a defect in the pulmonary capillary endothelium, immune related, that leads to bleeding, which leads to an accumulation of iron, which damages the lungs."

That's what I should have said.

Dr. Hartmann turned to me again. He asked, "What condition is sometimes associated with this condition?"

"I don't know." I scanned the ceiling, looking for some divine intervention. The rest of the entourage looked at Dr. Hartmann with the mad eyes of people in a mob anticipating a witch burned at the stake.

But Dr. Hartmann just frowned and said, "Miss Murtaugh?"

"Celiac disease."

"Correct. Mr. Spenser, have you checked for celiac disease?"

"No."

The crowd sensed blood. They could smell it.

"Mr. Spenser, how do you check for celiac disease?"

"I don't know."

Everyone but me was shaking their heads.

"Well, you'd better start knowing," said Dr. Hartmann. "Miss Murtaugh?"

"A duodenal biopsy, or if you want to do something less invasive..."

I didn't hear the rest. I walked away. No one stopped me. I was done.

I went to my locker, changed clothes, and drove home to my ninety-dollar-a-month apartment. Actually it only cost me forty-five dollars, because I shared the place with Jim Tucker, a fellow third-year student and my best friend. He wasn't home. Of course he wasn't home. He was at the hospital, learning how to be a doctor and doing what he was supposed to be doing.

I took a nap.

Late that afternoon Jim came home. He said, "I heard what happened. I went and talked to Dr. Callister. He told me to tell you that he wants to see you tomorrow at 6 a.m. in his office." Dr. Callister, a pathologist, was the faculty advisor for our class. He often won the shovel award for best teacher, the one who was best at "shoveling" knowledge into his students.

"Okay," I said.

"Anything I can do?"

"No, but thanks."

"Well, I'm your friend as well as your classmate, so just let me know."

"I know that."

Jim paused, debating whether to say anything or not. Then he said, "You know, it's not an either/or thing – you can make a living doing medicine and still do artistic stuff. You know I love music, but I plan to be a doctor and still play the piano."

"You aren't doing much piano playing these days."

"I know. But sometimes in life, I think you have to rearrange priorities. You have to do what you don't want to do for a while so that you can do what you want to do later. Right now, my priority is to get that M.D. degree. Later I can get back to music."

"But when does it end? After med school it will be internship and residency, with even more pressure. And then going into practice, with even more responsibility. Right now I'm just a med student, so what I think or do doesn't make much difference. Nobody *really* cares what I have to say. But when I'm a doctor, what I say or do *will* affect patients, so the stakes will be even higher. When do you get past the 'deferred gratification' stage, to actually live?"

"I don't know. But I don't see a reason not to see Dr. Callister."

Neither did I. I was getting kind of bored.

I showed up at Dr. Callister's office at 5:45 a.m. the next morning. I knocked on the door, no answer, but it was unlocked. I entered a reception area, which led to his office, which was locked. In the outer area six chairs were lined up next to one wall, with a table in the corner covered by a coffee maker, cups, coffee, sugar, and creamer. The other side of the room was dominated by a table with a twenty-gallon fish tank on top.

I gazed at the fish – black mollies, guppies, angel fish, and swordtails. I was fascinated by fish, ever since childhood when I wanted to be an ichthyologist when I grew up. I went to med school instead. I noticed one of the swordtails was swimming erratically, turning on its side from time to time. Some of the angel fish nipped at it, trying to wound it further. I grabbed one of the plastic coffee cups, dipped it into the tank, and rescued the injured reddish orange fish with the long tail.

Dr. Callister walked in. He was a tall sturdy man with short grayish brown hair, who liked the outdoors. In his free time he liked to canoe and white water raft the rivers of the south – the Ocoee, the Buffalo, and others – or go hiking, especially the Appalachian Trail.

"Are you the new janitor?" he asked.

"No. I'm just rescuing one of your fish." I told him what I did and why.

"Thanks. I can take that swordtail home and put him in an aquarium by himself for a while. Hopefully he can recover."

Dr. Callister unlocked the door connecting the reception area to his office. We entered and sat down, Dr. Callister behind his desk, me across from him. There wasn't a lot of room. A table with a microscope on top occupied one corner. There were a few file cabinets. Built-in bookshelves populated by textbooks and journals obscured the walls.

"Before we get started, let me show you this," he said. "Dr. Hartmann gave it to me yesterday afternoon." He handed me a handwritten note. It said:

> "Dear Dr. Hartmann,
>
> I want to pass on to you how much I appreciate the way a student, Jack Spenser, treated my son. It's hard to be a patient at a teaching hospital, because I sometimes get the feeling that the disease is more important than the patient, especially when that disease is a rare one, like my Thomas has.
>
> Anyway, Mr. Spenser was not like that, and I appreciate the time he spent with my son. I just wanted you doctors to know that.
>
> Mrs. Nancy Eatherly"

"I don't know what to say," I said.

"We don't get many letters like that. Usually the letters we get about our students and house staff are complaints."

"Well, he seems like a nice enough young man. I didn't expect him to be particularly outgoing and friendly. He's seventeen years old and will die soon of an incurable disease, and he doesn't understand why. I don't either."

"Well, enough about that. What's going on with you?"

I told him.

He nodded like he understood what I was trying to say. "So you want to write. What do you want to write about?"

That stopped me. I didn't say anything. I realized I didn't have much to say. I was twenty-three years old. I was about as deep and complex as a Mattel toy.

Dr. Callister said, "Well, maybe you ought to think this through before you do something crazy. This is your life we are talking about."

"To quote Faulkner 'The heart in conflict with itself.'"

"Fine, but if Faulkner were starting out today, I don't think he would have many readers."

"And I'm not Faulkner."

"Who is? Look, there's nothing wrong with writing, or any other kind of art for that matter – sculpture, painting, music…we need them, and they make life worth living. But we also need doctors to keep artists and their patrons alive when they get sick, so they don't die of…say, tuberculosis – like Thomas Wolfe, Walt Whitman, Robert Louis Stevenson and countless others."

"You have a point."

"Who do you want to read your books?"

"I haven't thought about it."

"Well, you'd better think about it. Again, we're talking about your life here, and, son, you haven't got but one, so don't waste it."

Neither one of us said anything. I knew this was one of those life-changing conversations, and how many of those happen in a life? Three? Six? Certainly no more than a dozen. Dr. Callister pointed to a book on his desk. The title was *Hematopathology*. He was the author.

"I do some writing," he said. "That book includes a new classification for malignant lymphomas, but I couldn't write about that until I did years of research to collect the data I needed. I think all writing is like that, even fiction. Before you write, you need data. And, son, you ain't got no data. You're not much more than a kid. You need some experiences, you need *to live*. Until that happens, what are you going to write about? Please don't write some bullshit 'coming of age' story, or a story about how mean your parents were, or tell about how your girlfriend broke your heart when she dumped you."

"You have a point."

"Exactly. There are enough stories like that out there. The last thing this world needs is another one. Get your M.D. degree. Get some data. And then write."

"Data? Getting my degree? I'm worried about getting through *this year*, passing my exams."

"I think you'll be okay."

"I may have to ask the school's permission to repeat the third year."

"I really doubt it will come to that. Besides, Ivory's already invested a lot of money in you, and they want you to graduate so you can become a rich alumnus and give money to the school. The last thing this school wants to do to you, a third-year student, is flunk you out. Maybe some-day you'll go out and win the Nobel Prize in medicine, or literature, and Ivory will be so proud of you."

"Now you're being sarcastic."

"I am. But still, I think you'll do okay. Right now, you've just hit a wall, which happens to a lot of students, probably more than you think. It's just your turn. Try to hang in there. Make it fun. Medicine really is fun, you know, if you don't get sidetracked by all the bullshit. Just take one day at a time, do the things you have to do that day, and I think you will do fine on your finals."

"And my writing?"

"What this world needs, and doesn't have, is a good writer who is a physician."

"Well, there was Anton Chekov."

"He's dead. Been dead a long time."

"Michael Crichton."

"He's not a real doctor. He's a science fiction writer."

"True. But he is a writer, and he did get an M.D. degree."

"Exactly! Which is what you need to do. Put off writing until you have something to write about. You're young. Get your degree, maybe practice medicine for a while, *and then* write. Or practice medicine *and* write – do both. Be a voice for medicine, for physicians, telling their stories. But first get your degree. And trust me, you'll pass your third-year exams."

I left Dr. Callister's office and went to the library to do what I should have done the night of Tom Eatherly's admission to the hospital – read the literature on idiopathic pulmonary hemosiderosis. Actually, from what I read, the prognosis wasn't all that bad. Eighty percent of patients with idiopathic pulmonary hemosiderosis lived into adulthood and had a normal life expectancy, and the prognosis was not related to how the patients do in childhood. Some, like Tom, had severe disease in child-hood, but then the disease seemed to calm down, and these patients went on to live a normal life.

Tom was eventually discharged from the hospital. I tried to see him whenever he came back to the hospital or was seen as an outpatient. As we hoped, he got better as he reached adulthood.

Last I heard, he was on medicines that controlled his disease. He became an accountant and got married – no kids last I heard. Even after I left Ivory, we stayed in touch for a while, especially during the NCAA basketball tournament. Each year Tom ran a bracket pool that I entered for several years. I never won, so I stopped playing.

Dr. Callister was right. I did pass my third-year exams, and I did get my degree, and I did practice medicine, for a long time actually. I got data, a lot of data. Then when I finished, I *could* write and tell the stories that only I could tell. *I could do that.* I'm doing that right now.

DR. BOB

May 1982

I will tell this story in the order in which the events occurred, although I was not present for some of them. I did not become involved in the narrative until the patient died. I can assure you, though, that everything that follows is true. The historical parts were general knowledge. Some of the clinical information was in the patient's medical record, or I learned it from the clinicians taking care of the patient. As for the rest of the story, I was there.

Dr. Bob McClain (everyone called him Dr. Bob) was descended from a long line of physicians. In the early 1800s Dr. Bob's great-grandfather Dr. James McClain settled in Siegeburg, Tennessee, and became the first physician. At that time Siegeburg was a town located about thirty miles west of Nashville, which was where those individuals who were too wild for Nashville ended up. Dr. James McClain rode on horseback throughout the town and countryside, delivering babies, setting broken bones, and practicing good frontier medicine. The most common treatment at the time was bloodletting, not stopping the bleeding, but doing the bleeding, which was thought to be a remedy for most illnesses. In fact, Dr. Bob still had his great-grandfather's porcelain bleeding bowl, with red and white stripes like you see at the barbershop. The bowl has a notch cut into it so that it could fit into the crook of the elbow where it collected blood dripping from a wound to the antecubital vein, the same vein we draw blood from today. The bowl had been passed on father to son until it reached Dr. Bob. It was one of his most prized possessions.

16

Dr. Bob's great-grandfather didn't pass on much else because he died at a young age. Siegeburg at the time attracted a notorious gambling element. Dr. James McClain was shot and killed by five gamblers in 1836 for allegedly cheating at cards. He was thirty-five years old. A local vigilante group caught and hanged the culprits.

Dr. Bob's grandfather Dr. Jerry McClain served in the Confederate Army during the Civil War under General Stonewall Jackson. He became quite adept at amputations – fingers, toes, legs below the knee, legs above the knee, arms…whatever was injured and dispensable. The South suffered from a lack of medical supplies, and many of the operations were done without anesthesia. Bacteria and concepts of antisepsis were unknown of course, so "laudable pus" was present at most wound sites. Unfortunately this laudable pus often turned into gangrene and death. After the war, Dr. McClain returned to Siegeburg and resumed his practice. He died of pneumonia in 1904 at the age of seventy.

Dr. Bob's father, Dr. Bill McClain, carried on the medical tradition. He made house calls, first on horseback, then by car. He started with a Model T Ford followed by Model A Ford. He carried a black bag filled with drugs, which, except for narcotics, were ineffective. But such futility was not restricted to Dr. McClain – it's pretty much the history of medicine. Until the discovery of penicillin and other antibiotics in the 1940s, medicines that actually worked, it was just as likely that a patient's encounter with a doctor would harm the patient as help the patient.

But Dr. Bill McClain wanted more than just a black bag. He wanted a hospital. So he built one. In 1919 he purchased a lot on the corner of Cambridge Avenue and Autumn Street, where he built a hospital and named it McClain Hospital. It consisted of one operating room, a dining room, a kitchen, and ten patient rooms. Dr. Bill McClain died of a stroke in 1935 at age sixty-six.

Dr. Bob was thirty-two years old when his father died. He carried on his father's medical practice as a combination surgeon, internist, and general practitioner. He did it all. Dr. Bob also inherited McClain Hospital and supervised its growth.

The first addition was in 1938 when another operating room was added, as well as an X-ray department, lab, and eight more patient rooms. A labor and delivery area, an emergency room, and a minor surgery area were built in 1941. In 1955 a pharmacy was put in.

McClain Hospital grew rapidly in the fifties and sixties, adding patient rooms as needed. By 1961 there were 74 patient rooms and four operating rooms. The X-ray department, laboratory, and emergency room area were expanded in the 1960s and early 1970s. By 1974 the hospital had 180 patient rooms.

At that point Dr. Bob sold McClain Hospital to Excel Healthcare Inc., a multibillion-dollar-sales company that was gobbling up independent hospitals throughout the country. The hospital was renamed Excel McClain Hospital. The exact terms of the sale were not disclosed, but Dr. Bob became the richest person in Siegeburg and the most prominent. Evidence of his philanthropy permeated the small town and much of Middle Tennessee.

By 1982 I had been in private practice of medicine/pathology for about four years. In 1974 I graduated from Ivory Medical School and then stayed there another four years to do my pathology residency. I stayed in Middle Tennessee to join the medical staff of Excel McClain Hospital and live in Siegeburg, Tennessee. By that time I was married to my wife, Sarah. We had two sons, Eric (six years old) and Matthew (four years old).

When I went to work each day, a portrait of Dr. Bob greeted me in the lobby of the hospital entrance. The picture occupied most of the wall behind the volunteers' desk. His eyes seemed to follow me as I made my way to the right, to my office in the lab.

That same portrait was in the main corridor where Eric went to school, a private school called McClain Christian Academy. He had donated the land on which the school is built, and gave a lot of money to help get it constructed. Every time I went to a school function – parent-teacher conference, PTO meeting, open house, sporting event…the visage of Dr. Bob smiled down at me.

I couldn't get away from the man. I went to a tennis camp one summer to try to improve my game and recapture some of my past glory. It was held at Newcomb College, a small Church of Christ school in Nashville. As I walked to the courts, I passed the newest building on the campus, and also the largest. I stopped to admire the architecture. Its many reflective windows gave it a futuristic appearance. The sign at the front said it was the McClain Science Hall. Was it named after Dr. Bob? No, it couldn't be, not here in Nashville. It was. After I finished my tennis sessions, I entered the building. In the lobby, on the wall straight ahead, that same smiling face of Dr. Bob greeted me. I read the plaque underneath, which had a message thanking him for his generous contributions that made McClain Science Hall possible.

I felt like I was living in Communist China during the Cultural Revolution, but instead of pictures of Chairman Mao, I saw Dr. Bob everywhere.

In this ubiquitous picture, Dr. Bob is smiling, and at first glance, he appears jovial, even kindly, with white hair and a ho ho ho Santa Claus look. But on closer examination, he does not appear completely benevolent. He holds a cigar in his right hand, not the best look for a physician. Also, when you look carefully, the smile is not open or generous, but guarded and calculating and even a little scary.

Siegeburg at the time was a suburban/rural community of about twenty-five thousand people. Of course Nashville and Siegeburg had both grown since the time of the first Dr. McClain, so they were no longer thirty miles apart. Interstate 40 connected the two, and there was only about fifteen miles of countryside separating the two communities. In every other direction there was nothing but the rolling hills and woods of Middle Tennessee for about a hundred miles. So Siegeburg was a suburb of Nashville, but it felt rural.

Excel McClain Hospital, where I worked, was a typical medium-sized hospital, a four-story structure. The Surgery Department was on the main floor and had four operating rooms. My office in the laboratory was across the hall. If I walked out of my office and turned right, the emergency room and X-Ray Department were a few steps away. I was right in the center of the action, where I wanted to be.

Dr. Bob was at the center of the action as well. He was seventy-nine years old but gave no indications that he would retire, ever. When he wasn't sleeping, he was at the hospital or in his office, working, and he worked fast. He could still do an abdominal exploratory staging operation for Hodgkin's disease in record time – take out the spleen, biopsy the liver, and do lymph node sampling in about thirty minutes, incision to closure. On his office days he could see about fifty patients in an afternoon – he knew how to clear out an office. A typical conversation with his office nurse, who was also thought to be his lover, went like this:

> Dr. Bob as he looks at a puncture wound on a patient's heel: "Give the patient a tetanus shot."
>
> Office Nurse: "But we're out of alcohol scrubs."
>
> Dr. Bob: "Give him a shot of penicillin as well, that should cover it. Next patient!"

His hospital rounds, however, were not so speedy. He showed his age as he walked through the hospital. He did rounds on his patients any time, day or night, whenever he could work them in. He shuffled slowly from one patient to the next, checking each one and taking a good while to get from patient A to patient B.

Coasting

Dr. Bob practiced medicine and performed surgery. Medicine is a profession, and surgery is a craft. Dr. Bob learned his profession and craft the same way any professional learns a profession or any craftsman learns a craft:

1. Master a large body of knowledge.
2. Acquire, practice, and apply specific skills.

This process is like pedaling a bicycle uphill. You pedal as hard as you can, seem to make little progress, then get close to the top of the hill, almost give up, but you are determined to make it. So you keep those wheels turning, and after years of study and hard work, you reach the top of the hill, and make it as an attorney, carpenter, plumber, artist, stay-at-home parent, professional golfer, investor, physician, or whatever else you are called to do.

Then you coast. It's downhill, and it's easy. You don't have to pedal your bike so much, if at all – just use the skills you have mastered to win legal cases, make furniture, fix the plumbing, paint pictures, manage a household, earn a living playing golf, make money, heal the sick and wounded – live your life.

And then you can coast for quite a while, maybe most of your adult life. An attorney learns the techniques that work and uses them over and over. A carpenter uses the same tools to the point they are an extension of his body. A plumber can fix a faucet in his sleep. An artist uses his or her skills to make paintings that only she can paint. A stay-at-home parent masters the household, and it starts to run itself. A professional golfer cuts back on practice time, but still wins tournaments. An investor finds his moneymaking niche and settles into it. A physician uses the same medicines over and over to build a practice of contented patients. A surgeon repeats a particular operation so often that it is no more difficult than tying his shoes, but to his patients he seems to be a demigod.

But coasting means you are going downhill. How do you know when you reach the bottom? For some professions, it's obvious:

1. An attorney starts losing cases, or falls behind.
2. A plumber or carpenter can't physically do the job anymore, or the technology changes. "Everything is computers now."
3. An artist loses her creativity, her vision.
4. The kids grow up. The spouse leaves or stays.
5. A professional golfer no longer wins tournaments.
6. An investor loses money.

And, a physician, well, how *does* a physician know he can't coast anymore, and he's reached the bottom?

William Jackson was a fifty-one-year-old man. His illness started in late April with fatigue, nausea, malaise, weakness, and a thirty-pound weight loss. The weight loss was not that big a deal, because he was a big guy and could afford to lose some of that load on his joints and heart. Mr. Jackson was a stoic guy and continued to do what he needed to do – drive a truck, hunt, and fish. As a general rule he stayed away from doctors. He lived with his symptoms for about a month, but then one weekend late in May he got sicker, with a fever of 103 degrees and a terrible headache. By Monday morning it was time to see Dr. Bob.

Dr. Bob was struggling. His wife of fifty-one years had recently died, and he was morose about that, and he wasn't sure why. It had been a loveless marriage for a long time. For about twenty-five years he had been carrying on a not-too-secret love affair with his office nurse. But when his wife died, Dr. Bob missed her a heck of lot more than he thought he would. Also the death of someone who had shared so much of his life seemed to focus his mind on the fact that he himself would die in the not-too-distant future, and that he would be the last of the line of McClain physicians. Dr. Bob's two sons had no interest whatsoever in medicine. One worked as a recruiter for the Army. The other was a real estate developer. In a few short years Dr. Bob would be dead, and the tradition of McClain physicians in Siegeburg would be over, which made him sad.

So Dr. Bob McClain was distracted on that Monday afternoon, and tired. William Jackson was one of sixty patients Dr. Bob saw that afternoon, part of the backlog of patients that occurred every Monday after the weekend. Dr. Bob had spent that morning doing surgery.

Dr. Bob shuffled into the examining room, smoking a cigar. He listened as the patient and his wife, Betty, described Mr. Jackson's symptoms of the past month, as well as the additional severe symptoms that had occurred over the weekend. Then Dr. Bob took out his trusty stethoscope, the same one he'd used since medical school at University of Tennessee, and he listened to William's heart and lungs. There was no rash on the patient's chest, and Dr. Bob did not see the rash on Mr. Jackson's arms and legs, because they were covered up with clothing. Dr. Bob smoked a cigar as he focused on the patient's breathing and heartbeat. Because of the cigar, Mr. Jackson coughed. Dr. Bob smiled.

That was it. History and physical completed. Dr. Bob said, "Well hell, William, I don't know exactly what you got, but it's some kind of infection. I'm going to give you some medicines that should take care of you."

Dr. Bob took a prescription pad out of the drawer and, as he was writing, said, "This one is for Phenergan, which should help with the nausea and cough and make you feel better."

Then he wrote out another prescription. Dr. Bob said, "This is an antibiotic, amoxicillin, which should get rid of any infection you got." He gave both prescriptions to Betty.

Dr. Bob exited and shuffled to his next patient.

The two prescriptions did not "take care" of William Jackson. The Phenergan and amoxicillin were ineffective; Dr. Bob might as well have used sugar water and salt pills. Over the next three days Mr. Jackson's symptoms got worse. His fever did not go away. He became weaker and weaker until he was so dizzy he could not stand up. By Thursday evening he was so sick that Betty was not sure he would live through the night. She dragged her good ole boy husband to the Excel McClain emergency room.

Dr. Steve Prescott was the internist covering the ER that night. He was about the same age as me, new to private practice after finishing his training at the University of Mississippi Medical Center. From what I could tell he was a good doctor. He was tall, about six feet six, and had played varsity basketball for Ole Miss. Dr. Bob was the person who had recruited him to come to Excel McClain Hospital. Steve's dad was a Methodist minister, and Steve felt called by God to come and help Dr. Bob. Dr. Bob encouraged this vision.

When Dr. Prescott examined his patient, it was obvious that Mr. Jackson was dying. His temperature was 105 degrees, pulse 140, and respiratory rate 28 – all way above normal. He struggled to breathe. His body was clearly fighting an infection, and losing. Steve noticed a rash, which now had spread from his extremities to cover the patient's whole body. The rash was a combination of red splotches like tattoos gone bad, and small pinpoint dots like wounds from a dart.

Steve asked about tick bites.

Mr. Jackson gasped, "Now that you mention it, I got ticks on me a week or two ago, when I went fishin' for bream at a friend of mine's pond."

Betty said, "I remember that. You brought home more ticks than fish."

Steve immediately made a diagnosis of Rocky Mountain spotted fever and started his patient on tetracycline, an antibiotic that is effective against the organism that causes Rocky Mountain spotted fever.

For the next five hours Steve watched a battle in Mr. Jackson's body between two sides.

On the one side was an infection, presumably Rocky Mountain spotted fever. The "Rocky Mountain" part of the name is a misnomer, because the disease is actually much more prevalent in the Appalachian

Mountain regions than the Rocky Mountains. The disease is certainly endemic in Tennessee. The organism that causes the disease, *Rickettsia rickettsii*, is spread by ticks. *Rickettsia rickettsii* infects cells lining blood vessels, which causes inflammation (a "vasculitis") with deleterious consequences. The vasculitis leads to hemorrhage, which shows up as a rash of the skin, but that hemorrhage also damages other organs like the kidneys, liver, brain, and any other structure in the body with blood vessels.

On the other side, fighting the infection, was Mr. Jackson's immune system and the tetracycline. His immune system tried to mitigate the effects of the infection by destroying the invading organisms and repairing the damage they caused. The tetracycline killed the *Rickettsia rickettsii* organisms, a valuable part of a hoped-for cure.

Steve sent Mr. Jackson to the Medical Intensive Care Unit, where he put his patient on 100% oxygen by mask, started an IV, and pumped in fluid as fast as possible. Monitors checked the patient's heart rate, blood pressure, respiration, and EKG pattern. Dr. Prescott tried to save his patient from this life-threatening illness.

Not to be. A few hours after reaching the unit, Mr. Jackson stopped breathing, turned blue, and his blood pressure dropped. Then his heart stopped. Steve knew his cardiology and immediately started cardiopulmonary resuscitation. Nothing helped. Mr. Jackson was pronounced dead at 1:47 Friday morning, four hours after seeing Dr. Prescott and four days after seeing Dr. Bob.

I came to work at 7 a.m. that Friday morning. Steve Prescott was waiting for me outside my office. Before I could sit down, he put a medical chart on my desk and said, "You have an autopsy to do."

I sat down. Steve remained standing. "Okay," I said.

"Let me tell you about it."

"Okay."

For ten minutes Steve talked rapidly, frowning and shaking his head as he told me the tragic medical history of Mr. Jackson. He finished by saying, "This patient had Rocky Mountain spotted fever, and by the time I saw him, it was too late to do anything about it. Dr. Bob should have made this diagnosis four days ago."

"What makes you so sure he had Rocky Mountain spotted fever?"

"The history…the tick bites…the clinical findings…the rash, the fever."

"Do you have positive serology for Rocky Mountain spotted fever?"

"No. Dr. Bob didn't order one. I had one drawn last night, but the results haven't come back yet. I'm sure the serology will be positive."

"Okay. It's a test we send out. It should come back in a day or two."

"The patient's wife is ticked off at Dr. Bob, doesn't understand why her husband is dead, and I don't know what to say to her."

Steve left my office, shaking his head.

Before I could take care of Mr. Jackson, who was dead, I had to take care of the living. I had several folders of microscopic slides from surgical pathology specimens to look at – tissue samples that I had to examine, interpret, and diagnose. Some were rush cases, a breast tumor biopsy and a prostate biopsy. The surgeons wanted the reports right away, so they could do any needed additional surgery as soon as possible, maybe even that morning or afternoon.

I had just started looking at slides through my microscope when Dr. Bob came into my office, without knocking. He was smoking a cigar.

"When are you going to do that autopsy on Mr. Jackson?" he asked.

"Around noon," I said.

"Let's do it now."

"I can't. I have to take care of these patients first." I nodded to the folders with slides I had to look at as soon as possible. "I already have clinicians calling me, wanting diagnoses."

Dr. Bob looked like I had given him something bad to eat.

"Anyway," I said, "what's the rush?"

"I just want it done with, get the family out of here, so they stop bothering me."

"Twelve noon is the earliest I can do it."

"I guess that will have to do. I'll meet you at the morgue."

He put the smoldering cigar in my trash can and shuffled out. I went back to looking through my microscope.

At noon I made it to the morgue, where Dr. Bob was waiting. We did the autopsy together. Dr. Bob may have slowed down on his feet, but he could operate as fast as ever. I appreciated the help.

The autopsy findings were minimal and nonspecific. What I saw could have been secondary to Rocky Mountain spotted fever, but it could also have been secondary to a lot of other things, like meningococcemia, various viral infections, and about a hundred other things that could cause inflammation. I saw the skin rash that captivated Dr. Prescott, and sampled some of the involved areas to look at under the microscope. I sampled all the organs – liver, lungs, brain...everything. I left untouched the face and other areas of the body that might be viewed by mourners. I collected blood and lung tissue for cultures. I also collected a tube of blood for Rocky Mountain spotted fever serology studies, which was about the only way I knew of to definitively diagnose the disease. The causative organism, *Rickettsia rickettsii*, does not grow on routine culture media, and even if it did, it is too dangerous to work with. Some scientists doing research on *Rickettsia rickettsii* have died of the disease after lab accidents.

I went to the sink to wash up before I changed out of my green scrubs. Dr. Bob was also wearing green scrubs. That was what he wore all the time. He was smoking a cigar.

"You know OSHA would have a fit about that cigar," I said.

Dr. Bob smiled.

Steve Prescott entered the morgue, which was a popular place on this Friday afternoon.

"Rocky Mountain spotted fever?" asked Steve.

Dr. Bob took the cigar out of his mouth. "No," he answered.

I said, "At this point I don't know what your patient died of. I saw a lot of nonspecific stuff – the lungs were congested with frothy fluid and blood, no wonder he had trouble breathing – but nothing specific or diagnostic."

Steve said, "He died of Rocky Mountain spotted fever. You got serology, didn't you?"

I nodded.

Dr. Bob smiled and left. Then so did Steve.

I sat at the small desk in one corner of the autopsy room and did clerical work. I filled out forms and dictated my findings, including the preliminary anatomic diagnoses and cause of death. My dictated findings would be transcribed and then go on the patient's medical record, with copies to the doctors who took care of the patient – Dr. Bob and Dr. Prescott. For preliminary anatomic diagnoses I included the skin rash, lung congestion, and other observations. For cause of death, I hesitated, but decided on "Unknown, Pending Further Studies."

Which I hated to do. I wanted to do my job, which was to diagnose a cause of death. But I needed more data, like the results of the cultures and the serology.

Finally I prepared the tissue samples for the histotechnologists to use to make microscopic slides to look at the next day. Maybe the microscopic examination would reveal some answers. I felt overwhelmed. Maybe I would be smarter tomorrow.

I finished up and cleaned up. I was alone. There was a body there, William Jackson's body, but William Jackson was long gone.

I went back to my office in the lab. I spent the rest of the afternoon taking care of patients – examining tissue specimens, answering clinicians' questions, looking at peripheral blood smears, solving laboratory problems as best I could…but I was troubled and had to work hard to concentrate.

I was relatively new in town and still trying to convince my colleagues that I knew what I was doing. My credibility was based on coming up with answers – whether the specimen sent to me had changes that were those of a tumor (and if so, whether it was benign or malignant), or inflammation (and if so, what was causing the inflammation – infection, trauma…) and so on. That's what I did. That's pretty much all I did, come up with answers.

But I didn't have the answer about what killed Mr. Jackson.

I was working on it, but whatever diagnosis I ended up with was going to please one physician, but not the other. A diagnosis of Rocky Mountain spotted fever would validate what Steve thought had killed the unfortunate Mr. Jackson, but that diagnosis would displease Dr. Bob. On the other hand, a diagnosis of something else, maybe something incurable, would be palatable to Dr. Bob, because then he could say there was nothing anyone could do…but Steve would not buy it.

I was most worried about the third option: that I never would come up with a definitive diagnosis of what killed Mr. Jackson. Sometimes patients just up and die, and we never do know why. There was a distinct possibility that I would end up just having to say "I don't know what caused the death of William Jackson."

Then nobody would be happy.

That night I dreamt that I was looking at slides with my microscope, and I couldn't figure out what had killed Mr. Jackson, and everyone was watching.

I wasn't any smarter the next day, a Saturday. I looked through the microscope at the slides of Mr. Jackson's tissues, the samples I had collected the previous day. It's a cliché to marvel at the working of a human body, and how beautiful it all is – but it's true. I gazed at the intricate mixture of cells and tissues of varying types and appearances, with a variety of functions and appearances. The organ samples were stained with only two dyes – blue hematoxylin and red eosin. But the differing proteins in each cell caused different staining characteristics that resulted in artwork, a beautiful array and variety of blues and reds with various shades, tints, and tones – like impressionist paintings.

The dominant change I saw was vasculitis, inflammation of the blood vessels. It was everywhere. Vasculitis was prominent in the skin and had caused Mr. Jackson's rash, but the vasculitis also affected the kidneys, liver, spleen…everywhere I looked. The vasculitis extensively involved the lungs with resultant hemorrhage and tissue injury. No wonder Mr. Jackson had struggled to breathe.

Unfortunately for me, vasculitis is not specific or diagnostic, so I still did not know what killed Mr. Jackson. Vasculitis is characteristic of Rocky Mountain spotted fever, but is also characteristic of numerous other conditions, which can also be associated with a fever and rash. Here is an incomplete list:

1. Viral infections
2. Bacterial infections, other than *Rickettsia rickettsii*
3. Toxins from cancer
4. Various drugs and medications
5. Autoimmune diseases like rheumatoid arthritis and lupus erythematosus

So I could not exclude Rocky Mountain spotted fever as a cause of Mr. Jackson's death, but neither could I exclude any of these other conditions as the etiology of his problems. I needed more information, something definitive.

Long, tall Dr. Prescott entered my office, looking like Lurch. "What did you find out about William Jackson?" he asked.

I pointed to the slides. "Vasculitis, highly abnormal, but nonspecific."

"Would you see that in Rocky Mountain spotted fever?"

"Yes."

"That's what he died of."

"I think you're right, but I have to prove it. I haven't done that."

"Can't you see the organisms under the microscope – what do you call them, the *Rickettsia*?"

"No. Not with my microscope. You need an electron microscope to do that."

"Can't you prove it with cultures?"

"No, the *Rickettsia* don't grow on the routine culture media we use, thank God, because if they did, that would be really dangerous. You need special conditions to grow *Rickettsia rickettsii*, and I think it's actually against the law to do that without a government permit."

"What's the next step, then?"

"Well, of course we've got serology pending. If that comes back positive, together with the characteristic vasculitis I'm seeing, and the clinical history – I will make a diagnosis of Rocky Mountain spotted fever."

"The patient's family wants to sue Dr. Bob for malpractice. I've let my malpractice carrier know what's going on, even though I didn't do anything wrong – they said, 'Thanks for letting us know.' I don't know what to tell the family."

"I don't have a cause of death."

"The cause of death was Rocky Mountain spotted fever, and Dr. Bob blew it. He should have started this patient on tetracycline the day he saw him."

"Well, I don't disagree with you about the diagnosis, but I need to prove it, and so far I can't."

"When will you get the serology back?"

"In a few days. I'll make some calls and see if I can get the reference lab to put a rush on it."

"It'll be positive."

"You're probably right."

"You'll let me know."

"Of course."

"Thanks."

About an hour later Dr. Bob came to my office. He wanted to know the same thing Steve did – why did William Jackson die?

I had the same answer for him that I did Steve. I didn't know.

Dr. Bob growled, "Dr. Prescott has been saying bad things about me to the family, to the wife, trying to get them to sue me for malpractice, because I didn't diagnose Rocky Mountain spotted fever. We still don't know that's what he had."

As Dr. Bob said this, he looked more hurt than mad. He continued, "After all I've done for Dr. Prescott – recruited him, welcomed him and his family to the community…" He shook his head gently, sadly.

"I'm waiting on the serology," I said.

"How will that help?"

"Well, if it's positive for Rocky Mountain spotted fever, that's the way I'm going to sign out the autopsy – death caused by Rocky Mountain spotted fever."

Dr. Bob lit a cigar and then walked away.

A few days later the serology tests came back *negative*. Both the serology Steven had collected when Mr. Jackson was admitted and the one I collected at the time of autopsy were negative for Rocky Mountain spotted fever.

Dr. Bob would be pleased. Dr. Prescott would be dismayed. I was neither.

Instead, I was mystified. I expected at least one of the tests to be positive. The principle of this serologic test is that the patient mounts an immune response to the infecting agent, in this case the *Rickettsia rickettsii*. Part of that response is the production of various proteins that are detected and show up as a positive serologic lab test for the *Rickettsia rickettsii*. That wouldn't happen right away, but Mr. Jackson had been sick for a month or so, with worsening symptoms the last week before his death. That was plenty of time, in my opinion, for the patient to convert from negative to positive serology. I didn't understand the negative results, which was totally *not* what I expected.

Sure enough, Steve was disappointed when I phoned him with the news. "I still think he had Rocky Mountain spotted fever," he said.

"Okay," I answered.

I phoned Dr. Bob and told him the serology results. Sure enough, he was pleased. He said, "I hope this shuts up Dr. Prescott."

"Okay," I answered.

I was stuck. I didn't have a diagnosis, which bothered me. The stakes weren't life and death, obviously – Mr. Jackson was deceased before I was even on the scene. But the stakes for me were huge.

I had to KNOW what really happened. So did Dr. Prescott and Dr. Bob and Mr. Jackson's family. It was my job to know what had happened, and I didn't. I was anxious. I wanted something definitive. I make my living by credibility, that when I render a diagnosis it is correct, what the patient really has, or in this case, what the patient really had.

I kind of agreed with Dr. Prescott – that Mr. Jackson died of Rocky Mountain spotted fever, but I couldn't prove it, and I wasn't sure of that diagnosis, not by a long shot. I was getting run down, anxious. I needed an expert to look at the case.

Where was there such an expert? Well, there was Dr. Callister, my teacher at Ivory. He was still there, long after I graduated from med school. Occasionally I sent him slides to look at for one reason or another. Some were just interesting or unusual cases that he could use to teach his students. Others were hard cases that I couldn't figure out on my own, and I needed his help – let's call them consults.

I hate to get consults. I want to think I have the brains, training, and experience to make my own diagnostic decisions. Also, if I have to ask for an "expert" opinion every time I get a difficult or challenging case, it's hard to know what good I'm doing.

On the other hand, if I never get help and just blunder on doing things I shouldn't be doing, I'll make mistakes, and that's not good either.

Striking a balance between these two competing principles is difficult. I don't think I'm alone in this regard. I think most physicians struggle to strike a balance between getting help and not getting help. Non-physicians as well.

I had not lived in Siegeburg very long. I didn't have a reputation for excellence to fall back on if I messed up this case, which I was on the verge of doing. I had no history at all with Dr. Prescott, who was new to Siegeburg, and he had no idea if I was a good pathologist or not. The evidence I had presented to him so far was that I didn't know what I was doing.

So I decided to go to Dr. Callister for help. I dictated a cover letter to him. I gathered the clinical history notes and my autopsy results so far, including the negative serology. I put rubber bands around the folders holding the microscopic slides. Then I put the paperwork and slides in a big brown envelope addressed to Dr. Callister.

By that time it was midafternoon. The lab was reasonably quiet, so I drove to Ivory Medical Center. It was 4 p.m. when I found Dr. Callister. He was in a small conference room dominated by a relatively large rectangular table. He was seated along with his entourage of six medical students and house staff, all of them looking through the eyepieces of a large teaching microscope, which covered much of the table. The teaching microscope was designed so that everyone looking through it saw the same thing.

Dr. Callister saw me enter the room and looked up. His eyes were red, and his countenance had a washed-out pale appearance. I told him that he looked tired.

He smiled and said, "Well, Jack, I was feeling pretty good until you came along. Now I don't feel so good."

I laughed. I told him why I was there bothering him and gave him the brown envelope. He opened it and took out a few of the microscopic slides and started looking at them through the teaching microscope. I sat down and adjusted the lenses to my eyes so I could look through the microscope and see the slides along with everyone else in the room. We were optically connected to each other, in our very own microscopic world. "What's your impression?" he asked.

"I think it's a vasculitis, like what you would see with Rocky Mountain spotted fever."

"Yeah, but you can see vasculitis in a lot of other things, viral infections for example."

Dr. Callister looked at the slides for a few more minutes, then said, "Look, we have about six bone marrows we have to sign out right away, so I'm going to have to put your case aside, get back to it later. I'll give you a call."

"No rush," I said. It was an autopsy case. The patient sure wasn't in a rush.

"I will give you an answer," said Dr. Callister, "and it will be definitive."

Dr. Callister phoned me two days later, and his answer was not definitive. "Your case is too hard," he said.

"I don't send you my easy ones."

"Right. Well, send me an easy one next time – give me a break."

We discussed the pathologic findings, which were as nonspecific to him as they were to me.

I asked, "Could it be Rocky Mountain spotted fever?"

"Maybe, but I don't think so."

"Why?"

"Didn't you say the serology was negative?"

"Yeah, but that doesn't rule out the disease."

"Sure makes it less likely though. I don't think you have enough here to call it."

"Can I do some additional tests, like electron microscopy or something definitive? I hate to not know."

"Dr. James Gresham, over at the University of North Carolina, is working on an immunofluorescence test for Rocky Mountain spotted fever."

Immunofluorescence works like this. A chemical reacts with what you're looking for in tissue, in this case *Rickettsia rickettsii*, which sets off a chain of chemical reactions with the end result being fluorescence, i.e., light, which can be seen with an immunofluorescence microscope. If the *Rickettsia rickettsii* organism is there, light shows up. If not, everything stays dark. Neat.

I said, "I didn't know there was an immunofluorescence test for Rocky Mountain spotted fever."

"Well, it's not commercially available. Dr. Gresham is doing research on it. But he tells me it really works. In this case, though, I think it's a waste of time."

"Just call me Don Quixote and humor me."

Dr. Callister gave me Dr. Gresham's address and phone number.

"You doing any writing?" he asked.

"No."

"You need to."

I immediately gave Dr. Gresham a call. I didn't know the man, but he seemed really nice on the phone. He said he would be happy to help me out. I asked him about doing electron microscopy on the tissues. I'd seen photographs of *Rickettsia rickettsii* of the organism as it appeared with EM.

Dr. Gresham said immunofluorescence would be better. The magnification is higher with EM, but as he said, "With EM you're looking at one particular ear of corn, whereas with immunofluorescence, I'm looking at the whole cornfield."

I mailed Dr. Gresham what he needed and hoped he would come up with the answers. I really wanted to know what had happened to Mr. Jackson. That's why I went into pathology. I wanted to know.

I phoned Steve and told him what I was doing. I said, "I am sending the case to the world's expert on Rocky Mountain spotted fever. If he can't tell me the answer, no one can, and we'll never know what happened."

Steve replied, "That's what I'll tell the family. I think they will be satisfied with that, that we've done all we can."

Tuesday of the following week I attended the monthly meeting of the Internal Medicine Department. About fifteen doctors showed up. As a pathologist, I'm not really a member of the department, but the internal medicine docs like me to show up to answer any questions that come up about the lab or pathology. Dr. Bob was also there – I wasn't sure why – maybe because his name was still on the hospital signage, and he wanted to know what was going on. Plus, it was a noon meeting with lunch, and Dr. Bob liked the fried catfish.

He didn't like much else about that meeting. Part of the agenda each month was a death conference, which was exactly what it sounds like. Any patient's demise that happened on the medical ward was reviewed by the internal medicine department, to make sure that everything that could have been done was done. And if mistakes were made, everyone could learn from those mistakes and do better in the future.

Usually the discussions were perfunctory. The typical internal medicine patients admitted to the hospital were chronically ill with a host of life-threatening diseases, including diabetes, end-stage kidney disease, heart failure, emphysema, and cancer – any of which could cause the death of the patient. Usually the question at the time of death was "How did the patient live so long?" not "Why did the patient die?"

That was not the case with Mr. Jackson, however. He was only fifty-one years old, and in good health until his final illness and death. So the members of the department stopped paying attention to their desserts and listened as Steve Prescott presented the clinical findings and brief hospital stay of Mr. Jackson. Steve delivered this information in a dry flat technical manner, almost a monotone. He finished by saying that his diagnosis and interpretation was that the patient died of Rocky Mountain spotted fever.

I wanted him to finish there, but Steve, son of a Methodist minister, continued with some fire and brimstone: "This death could have been prevented. Dr. Bob here saw the patient in his office four days before his admission to the hospital and should have made the correct diagnosis and started the patient on tetracycline. Instead he gave the patient Phenergan and amoxicillin, which were ineffective, and by the time I saw the patient, it was too late to save him."

Dr. Bob stopped eating. He lit a cigar. He said, "That's pretty strong language. What makes you so sure he had Rocky Mountain spotted fever?"

"The clinical history, the tick bite, the clinical findings, the fever, the rash…"

"But the serology for Rocky Mountain spotted fever was negative. How do you explain that?"

Everyone was silent. Finally Steve said, "I guess this was an early stage of the disease, and there hadn't been enough time for the serology to turn positive."

Dr. Bob said, "But you said the patient had been sick for a month, for over a month. That should have been plenty of time for the test to turn positive. I don't think you've proved that the patient had Rocky Mountain spotted fever at all."

Steve turned to me. "What do you think, Jack? You did the autopsy."

Everyone turned to me. I had the attention of the whole room. Even the kitchen staff clearing the plates and glasses stopped to listen.

I said, "I don't know what this patient died of. I sent the case to Dr. Gresham of the University of North Carolina, the world's expert on Rocky Mountain spotted fever. I'm waiting for his report."

Everyone shrugged, not at all impressed with my acumen. I wish I were smarter. I wish I were better.

A couple of weeks went by, and I didn't hear from Dr. Gresham. Dr. Gresham was doing this work for us for free, so I didn't pester the man. For the record, I wasn't getting paid for my work either. Autopsies were perhaps the only free service at a hospital at the time, which, when you think about it, was understandable.

However, there are timing requirements to get autopsy reports done, which are set by various accrediting agencies. Of course that makes sense – there can be some urgency in making diagnoses. For example, if the patient who died had some contagious disease like tuberculosis or meningitis, that diagnosis has to be made official reasonably quickly so measures can be taken to prevent the spread of the disease. A pathologist can't fiddle around for months while an epidemic spreads throughout the community. And as a general rule, it's good to have deadlines, to make sure the work that needs to be done is in fact done.

So after two weeks went by, I was required to write up Mr. Jackson's autopsy report, which I was not particularly proud of. I listed my findings, which were mainly related to the vasculitis. For final cause of death, I put "PENDING FURTHER STUDIES, SEE FINAL SUMMARY." In that final summary I wrote that the final cause of death was pending further studies, including the report of Dr. Gresham, and that those results would be included in an addendum report. Copies of what I wrote went into the patient's chart, as well as to the doctors who took care of the patient – Steve Prescott and Dr. Bob.

A few days later Steve Prescott saw me walking from my office to the cafeteria for some breakfast. He came over to tell me that he saw my report. He asked when I would hear back from Dr. Gresham. I said I didn't know. I was saying that a lot lately.

I didn't hear anything from Dr. Bob or anyone else.

Four weeks later I finally received a letter from Dr. Gresham. It said:

"Dear Dr. Spenser,

Examination of the tissues from your case (AM-82-09) revealed numerous *Rickettsia rickettsii.* The lungs in particular had a very heavy infection, which correlates with the respiratory symptoms. The negative serologic result indicates an early phase of Rocky Mountain spotted fever. Therefore, the month-long illness of this patient was probably not due to the Rocky Mountain spotted fever infection. However, Rocky Mountain spotted fever evidently did cause this patient's illness during the last week of his life, which led to his death. I hope these results are helpful.

James Gresham, M.D."

Case solved! Mr. Jackson died of Rocky Mountain spotted fever. I had a tremendous sense of satisfaction, and I was reminded again why I love pathology. This information was not going to help Mr. Jackson, obviously, but it would help others, including, perhaps, his family. It would be a relief, I think, for them to know what had happened. Also, I believe there is something intrinsic to the human spirit to seek knowledge, and TO KNOW, even if there is no immediate tangible benefit. We discovered what killed Mr. Jackson. To summarize:

With his immunofluorescence studies, Dr. Gresham saw the organisms that caused Rocky Mountain spotted fever, especially in the lungs. No wonder Mr. Jackson had had trouble breathing. The Rocky Mountain spotted fever serology was negative, because the patient died before his body could mount the kind of response that would show up in the tests. The patient's month-long illness was a side issue, unrelated to anything really, probably one of those lingering viral infections that are not life-threatening, but hard to get over, but he would have recovered from that. Unfortunately, before that could happen, Mr. Jackson became infected with the *Rickettsia rickettsii,* and the last week of his life was dominated by Rocky Mountain spotted fever. It killed him.

I dictated this new information into an addendum report, and for cause of death, I put down ROCKY MOUNTAIN SPOTTED FEVER. This addendum would be distributed to the usual suspects.

I phoned Dr. Prescott and told him the news.

"I told you," he said.

"Yes, you did."

"Thanks for sticking with it and not giving up."

Steve wanted copies of everything – my correspondence with Dr. Gresham, Dr. Gresham's report, my final autopsy report, including the addendum – everything, which he wanted to pass on to his malpractice insurer, which he did. Steve later told me that the insurance people said, "Thank you very much." Dr. Prescott did not get sued about Mr. Jackson's death.

No one did.

Why did no one get sued for malpractice? I don't know. My first rule of lawsuits is that no one knows anything, so there's that. But just consider:

Dr. Prescott didn't get sued, because he did nothing wrong.

But, but, but Dr. Bob should have gotten sued! He messed up. He didn't see the rash. He didn't ask about ticks. He didn't prescribe the right medicines. He didn't, he didn't…He committed malpractice.

And I say, not so fast. He did make mistakes. But ask yourself, do you really want that to be the standard of malpractice? Mistakes? Do you want that to be the standard in your work, your life, perfection?

Just consider:

1. It took me weeks to make the correct diagnosis, and I used every resource I had, some that Dr. Bob didn't have, like a total examination at the time of the autopsy.
2. Even Dr. Callister was unsure of the diagnosis, the smartest man I know. He wasn't just unsure that the disease in question was Rocky Mountain spotted fever. He was convinced it *wasn't* Rocky Mountain spotted fever.
3. I needed the help of the world's expert on the disease to finally make the correct diagnosis.

All of these facts were known by the patient's family, and all of these facts would have been known to a potential jury, and most importantly, those facts would have been quickly apparent to the plaintiff's attorney, who might not have wanted to waste a lot of time and energy on a contingency malpractice suit, which he had a good chance of losing.

And it's another cliché but true: nothing, including a successful malpractice suit, was going to bring William Jackson back to life.

So set potential malpractice aside. Now, the separate issue: Did Dr. Bob make a mistake?

Dr. Prescott sure thought so. So did I.

What did Dr. Bob think? He never told me.

What did Dr. Bob do? I do know that. Here's the rest of the story:

I phoned Dr. Bob and told him about Dr. Gresham's report, and how I had signed out the autopsy as death due to Rocky Mountain spotted fever. Dr. Bob didn't say anything. I'm sure that he had a cigar in his mouth. He just grunted and hung up. I suspect the cigar never left his mouth.

I phoned Dr. Callister and told him Dr. Gresham's findings. Dr. Callister was surprised. He said, "I did not think your patient had Rocky Mountain spotted fever."

"No one's perfect," I said.

"Good thing you didn't listen to what we at this great academic center thought about the case."

I laughed. "But you pointed me in the right direction – to Dr. Gresham."

"Put it in your book," he said.

"One of these days…"

Dr. Callister hung up.

From then on I didn't see much of Dr. Bob. Neither did anyone else. He stopped admitting patients to the hospital, referring them instead to Dr. Prescott. He stopped doing surgery. If one of his patients needed an operation, he referred the patient to Dr. Mitch Thornburg, one of the younger surgeons.

Dr. Bob cut his office hours way back. He continued to see patients who had been with him a long time, but closed his practice to new patients. Most of Dr. Bob's patients were as old or older than he was, so his practice gradually but literally died off.

Dr. Diane Murtaugh, my medical school classmate, and now a pediatrician in Siegeburg, saw more of Dr. Bob than I did. She told me that Dr. Bob had been spending a lot of time at the Siegeburg Church of Christ, which was unusual for him. His work had always been his religion. Now he was attending church every Sunday morning and Wednesday evening and showed up for all those potluck suppers with that great fried chicken. My oldest son told me that he often saw Dr. Bob eating lunch at McClain Christian Academy, especially on Fridays when they served fish and chips.

In the February 1983 issue of the *Tennessee Medical Association Journal* I saw this Letter to the Editor:

"Excel McClain Hospital

Siegeburg, TN 38017

Dear Sir,

I have been continuously practicing medicine in this state for 55 years, which to my knowledge is longer than anyone else. If you have been practicing in this state longer than I have, I would like to hear from you.

Bob McClain, M.D."

Over the next couple of months Dr. Bob continued his minimal office practice, and I rarely saw him in the hospital. One Friday early in May, a year after Mr. Jackson's illness and death, I was really busy – looking at slides, taking care of lab issues, doing consults in the operating room...a typical busy Friday at the hospital. So I was late getting to the Doctors Lounge for some lunch, and I got there just before it closed. Dr. Bob was there, alone, smoking a cigar. I asked him if I could join him. He took the cigar out of his mouth, smiled, and nodded.

It was the first time I'd seen Dr. Bob in a long time. I was glad to see him. I asked how he was doing, and he said he was doing good. We caught up with each other's business.

I said, "That letter you wrote to the state medical journal, the one asking if anyone in the state had been practicing longer than you?"

"Yeah."

"Did anyone respond? Did anyone top you?"

"No."

"Impressive."

And that's where we left it.

Dr. Bob waited until the end of the month. Then he closed his office and retired. He stopped coasting and got off the bike. I never saw him again.

BLOOD IS A SPECIAL JUICE

August 1987

Collecting bone marrow is like drilling for oil – it's nice to have a gusher. Sid Barksdale, my patient, a thirty-eight-year-old man, was lying facedown on his hospital bed. I felt the geologic/anatomic landmarks of his right hip, looking for the right posterior superior iliac spine, which is a bone that sticks out like a spur, as if it were made for sampling bone marrow. That is, if you can find it.

You can also get bone marrow from the sternum, which is easier to find – just feel the middle of the front of your chest, and there it is, the breast bone – you can't miss it. I could easily stick a needle in there and suck out some bone marrow. Unfortunately, it's not that hard to poke the needle through the sternum to puncture the heart, aorta, or lungs – things that you really don't want to puncture. Physicians have done that, with fatal consequences – a therapeutic misadventure if you will.

So the region of the iliac crest, the hip bone, is a relatively safe region to operate in. There is a downside to this course of action, though. That posterior superior iliac spine is tiny and hard to locate, so there have been times that I've poked the aspiration needle and biopsy needle into the region, and "missed" it. Then I've had to try again and again and again. The patient does not enjoy feeling like a pincushion, and there's the mounting frustration of me, my assistant, the anesthetist, and the operating room nurse with my inability to get the operation done – the whole thing can become a real pain in the ass. Such an outcome is particularly likely if the patient has a lot of fat in the area, so that I can't find my usual anatomic landmarks, which are obscured by fat. If that happens, it's like driving in the dark with no headlights.

Fat was not an issue with Sid Barksdale. He was in great shape. Actually, I thought Sid Barksdale was a pretty good-looking guy, as guys go – maybe because he was such a contrast to me. We were both in our thirties at the time, but otherwise we were quite different. Sid was tall, about six feet four. I was short, about five feet five. Sid had straight blond hair, and even in the hospital it was nicely combed, not a hair out of place. My hair was coal black, wiry, curly, and impossible to comb. My steady state look at the time was that of a deranged-appearing Albert Einstein, without the brainpower. Sid's eyes were pale gray, and he didn't need glasses. My eyes were brown, but no one noticed because I wore glasses all the time. Sid back then had the athletic build of a small forward in the NBA, and I looked like one of the shorter members of the pro golf tour, with a little more of a gut.

I knew Sid Barksdale pretty well, actually, which was unusual for me – to know one of my patients. Usually I didn't. First of all, as a pathologist, a doctor in the laboratory, I examine specimens, not patients, which is the way I like it – I like specimens better than patients. So for the most part, I didn't meet the patients I took care of, I just examined their specimens.

However, I do collect my own bone marrow specimens, so at those times I actually meet real live patients. Even then, though, that patient encounter is usually a onetime meeting, with someone I've never seen before and will never see again. I don't know that many people.

But I knew Sid Barksdale, had known him for a long time. We went to college together at Sewanee, and we both were on the varsity tennis team. Sid was a better player than I was, not much better, but enough. Sid was number one singles, and I played number three singles. My senior year, our team won the Conference Championship, with both Sid and I winning individual championships as well, Sid at number one, me at number three.

It always seemed to me that things came easy for Sid. He was the best at tennis, with minimal practice because he was so tall and athletic. I had to practice hard, because I was short and not as athletic. He got good grades, as good as mine, with seemingly much less effort, or no real effort at all. Part of the reason for this may have been the difference in coursework. Sid took pre-law courses like history, English, political philosophy…courses that I thought were a bunch of bullshit, in the sense that to get good grades, all you had to do was write bullshit essays about bullshit topics and write bullshit term papers about bullshit subjects. In contrast I was taking premed courses, hard subjects like organic chemistry, physics, calculus – subjects that required time, concentration, and effort. The only science course Sid took was political science.

I felt the top of the right iliac crest, that bone you can feel on the side of your hip, which extends like a bulwark to protect and surround those vital pelvic structures. From the back edge of the iliac crest, I went two fingerbreadths toward the midline and two fingerbreadths down and marked that place on the skin with a marking pen, leaving a black dot. That's where the posterior superior iliac spine was supposed to be. I pressed hard with my fingertips to see if I could feel it, and I could. So far, so good. I scrubbed the area with Betadine and alcohol and then covered up the sterile area with drapes, leaving only the black dot exposed. I was ready to go.

What really made me jealous of Sid, though, was his success with women. I didn't have many dates in college, maybe half a dozen the entire four years I was there. Maybe not that many. Sid had that many dates over the course of a month, or less. It just wasn't fair.

And then there was this time I asked Carole Mueller, a nursing student, for a date. I'd had a crush on her for a long time, and it took a lot of courage for me to ask her out. One autumn evening I ran into her at the library, and I asked her to go to a movie Saturday night – *Love Story* – I'd heard it was pretty good. She declined in a perfunctory fashion, said she had other plans, in a tone that indicated she didn't care if I disappeared into a Buddhist monastery for the rest of my life.

That hurt, but wasn't that big a deal, because that kind of thing happened to me a lot. I was a boring person back then, probably still am. Looking back, I'm amazed I had any dates at all.

But what happened later that evening really hurt. After studying at the library for a few hours, I went to my dorm. There was only one phone on the floor, and Sid was on it, talking to Carole Mueller. He motioned me to hold up. I couldn't help but overhear the short conversation as I waited. He asked her for a date to a frat party happening *that very same*

Saturday that that she told me she had other plans. I overheard her say, "Yes, sounds great." She sounded quite happy.

Sid went over the logistics of the coming event, hung up the phone, and turned to me. He wanted to chat a minute and catch up and see how I was doing – which was pretty lousy. I felt totally humiliated, but I didn't feel like telling him why. It was one of those times in life that clearly separated a winner from a loser, and it was obvious which category Sid was in and which category I was in.

The anesthetist slowly administered propofol through Sid's IV to put him to sleep. To make sure Sid felt no pain, I also used a lot of local numbing medicine. I used a needle and syringe to squirt 1% xylocaine into the skin, soft tissue, and outside of the bone. When I reached the bone my needle bumped up against the posterior superior iliac spine. Excellent! I knew exactly where I was, which was right where I wanted to be. I pulled the needle out and waited for the xylocaine to take effect.

Carole Mueller became Mrs. Sid Barksdale, and they had two kids, both girls – Kim, ten years old, and Carey, who was twelve. Carole's father was president of Siegeburg Bank and Trust, the largest bank in the county. Sid went to the University of Tennessee Law School, passed the bar exam, but then never really practiced law. Instead he went to work at his father-in-law's bank. Carole finished her nursing training and went to work in the endoscopy suite of Excel McClain hospital. It was a day job, so she could still get the kids off to school in the morning and be home when the kids got home.

Sid was a natural finance guy. He liked making loans, helping people out – helping them buy homes, start businesses, or whatever they needed money to do. He never missed a ribbon cutting for a new business or store that he helped finance. The loans Sid made tended to work out because he was a good judge of people. Also his investments did well. He had a knack for discerning what was a good business and what was a bad business, and invested accordingly. Sid believed in the virtues of saving money and investing it. Simply put, he understood money. Most people don't. Sid had it made. He sat in a nice temperature-controlled office that smelled nice, with windows overlooking a garden park with a pond. He shuffled papers, went to meetings, and made phone calls. How hard is that? With relatively little real work, he made a lot of money.

In contrast, I worked my butt off for the money I earned. I was on my feet a lot – running back and forth to the operating room, standing at a dissecting table, doing occasional autopsies, and, well, collecting bone marrow specimens. When I wasn't on my feet, I spent long hours sitting in an office with no windows, looking through a microscope, which made my back and neck hurt, as well as my hands and wrists. Every pathologist I know has had carpal tunnel syndrome surgery. Look, I know what I was doing wasn't like pouring cement all day, but the job took a toll on my body, and I'm not even going to get into the fumes I breathed from formaldehyde, xylene, and the other chemicals we used in the lab.

And when it came to savings and loans, well, I was definitely on the getting-a-loan side. I used student loans to get through college and med school and got a mortgage to buy a house. I was a long way from paying them off.

I used the sharp point of a scalpel to puncture the skin and make a hole about the size of a BB. Blood filled the wound the way a blush fills a face. I applied pressure with a couple of four-by-four sponges. When the bleeding stopped, I saw the yellow soft subcutaneous fat, which shined like a field of wheat in the sun. I slowly advanced the Illinois needle through the skin and fat, which I could see, to the muscle and bone that I could not see. Most of the procedure was done by touch and feel, which I hated. I like to SEE.

Sid was young, so his bones were healthy and hard, with the texture of rigid driftwood. It took all my hand, arm, and shoulder strength to press the needle through the outer bone into the bone marrow. The xylocaine worked, and so did the propofol. Sid was feeling no pain.

But politics, not banking, was Sid's real love, and he was good at it, a natural. When he turned thirty, he was elected to represent Siegeburg County in the state legislature. He was re-elected every two years by landslides. Last spring break, while the legislature was in session, my oldest son, Eric, worked for Sid as a page. Every morning Eric walked on the floor of the House and brought Sid the morning paper and coffee. Throughout the day Eric delivered written messages from Sid to other representatives and ran any other errands as needed. By the end of the two weeks, Eric idolized Sid Barksdale. And with good reason – Sid was an outstanding representative. Sid thought he could *kind of* help people as a banker, but he could *really* help people as a politician.

For example, there was this couple who consistently contributed money to Sid's election campaigns, not a lot, but every little bit helped. Then two years ago their son got arrested for dealing drugs. He was duly tried, convicted, and sentenced to five years in prison at Brushy Mountain State Penitentiary in a remote part of Eastern Tennessee, over two hundred miles from Siegeburg and hard to get to. The parents asked Sid: Is there was any way their son could be transferred to the State Prison in Nashville, which would make it easier for them to visit him, stay connected, and give him hope?

The answer was yes. Sid made the phone calls and wrote the letters to make it happen. Sid told me about the story one evening when he sat next to me at a retirement banquet for a friend of ours. "Jack," he said, "I was happy to help out. The young man is still going to do the time, but his family can visit him and stay involved in his life, and maybe he will have a better chance at rehabilitation."

I advanced the Illinois needle inside the iliac crest bone. This next part of the procedure, aspirating bone marrow, i.e., sucking out the bone marrow, was going to hurt. Actually it was going to hurt like hell. The skin, soft tissue, and outside of the bone were bathed in local anesthetic, so no pain there. However, the inside of the bone, where the bone marrow was located, wasn't numbed at all. The Illinois needle was attached to a 20 cc syringe. I drew back the plunger and waited to see what happened.

Sid wasn't obnoxious about his luck or his success. He was very matter of fact about it, seemed to take it for granted, like a nice day or good health. Of course, this too made me jealous, because I had to work hard for any success I had, and I never took anything for granted.

I regarded Sid as lucky, even when he had bad luck. Take this present admission to the hospital, which in a way was fortuitous. Sid had been driving alone in his Mercedes sedan Saturday evening on his way home from the monthly Siegeburg County Democratic Party meeting. A seventeen-year-old lad driving a Ford pickup was evidently distracted by his girlfriend sitting close next to him, so he didn't see the red light at the intersection until he hit Sid's Mercedes on the driver side.

Miraculously, no one was hurt too badly, just some bumps and bruises – no blood on any of them. However, as a precaution, everyone involved went to the Excel McClain emergency room. Dr. Tom Bruno, the orthopedic surgeon on call, ordered the appropriate X-rays and lab tests to make sure no one had suffered any serious injuries. The young man and his girlfriend were sore but otherwise okay, so their parents came and picked them up.

However, Sid's bumps and bruises kept getting bigger and bigger – rapidly. The nurses were concerned. So was Dr. Bruno. The X-rays were normal, but when he checked the lab work, he noted that Sid's platelet count was low – 25,000. Anything less than 150,000 is abnormal. Platelets are tiny components in blood, much smaller than red blood cells. Platelets function to stop bleeding by starting a clot, a very important part of the process. Since Sid's platelets were low, his bumps and bruises – caused by bleeding – continued. In fact, as time went on, the bleeding worsened. So, in a way, the auto accident was good luck, calling attention to his low platelets before the situation got critical. If Sid's platelet count had been much lower, he would have had serious spontaneous bleeding rather than bleeding related to trauma – something like a brain hemorrhage, which would have been catastrophic.

Surprisingly, the low platelet count was the only abnormal lab result. Everything else was normal. Sid was not anemic. His white blood cell count was normal. Only his platelet count was out of line. That was weird. So Dr. Bruno called in Dr. Aaron Rickert, a hematologist-oncologist, to take over. This was a hematology case, not an orthopedic case.

Dr. Rickert was puzzled as well. An isolated abnormality, the low platelet count, was rare, especially in someone like Sid, so young and healthy. He wasn't diabetic, hypertensive, or depressed. Various medications can have a side effect of causing low platelets, but Sid took no medicines whatsoever – didn't need 'em. Dr. Rickert ordered platelet transfusions to get Sid out of the low platelet danger zone. He also ordered a bone marrow exam to be done by Jack Spenser, M.D., the pathologist – me.

This next part was going to hurt, even though the anesthetist kept Sid asleep, and I had numbed up everything I could with the xylocaine. There's no way to make the inside of the bone numb, so when I drew back on the plunger, Sid groaned in pain, even though he was uncon-scious from the propofol. I know it sounds like I'm deranged, but I was pleased with Sid's pain, because it reassured me that the needle was in the right spot. It's a brutal fact that the best sign of a successful bone marrow collection effort is that it hurts like hell as it happens. The bone marrow gushed into the syringe, like hot water from a geyser. In the bone the bone marrow is interspersed in fat, so I saw little glistening yellow-ish/gray particles of fat admixed with bone marrow, so the specimen looked like shiny blood. After collecting 5 ccs of bone marrow, I replaced the syringe with another one and collected another 5 ccs. I repeated the process until we had collected four syringes of bone marrow. My assistant triaged the samples. One would be used for smears; they would be stained in the laboratory, and I would look at the smears with my micro-scope to examine the morphology of the cells. A second sample would be used for a clot section; it would be processed overnight into micro-scopic slides that I would also look at with my microscope to examine the morphology of the specimen. The third sample would be sent to a specialty laboratory for cytogenetic studies (i.e., examination of the chro-mosomes of the cells, which might give clues to a diagnosis), and flow cytometry (which is used to study cell types, which might also render clues to a diagnosis). The fourth specimen was a spare sample (just on principle).

I pulled out the Illinois needle, which did not hurt Sid. In fact, the painful part, pulling back on a plunger, was over. The rest of the proce-dure just involved pressure, and that's all Sid felt. I pressed the Jamshidi (rhymes with damn sheety) needle into the same place to collect a piece of bone as well as bone marrow. I pulled out the needle and removed a 15 mm piece of bone and bone marrow, which I put into formalin. It would be used for morphology, like the smears and clot section.

While Sid was coming out of the anesthesia and waking up, I used four-by-four sponges to put pressure on the wound for twenty minutes to make sure the bleeding stopped. With Sid's low platelets, that was no sure thing. I checked and didn't see a speck of blood, so I taped on a pressure dressing.

"How did it go?" asked Sid.

"Could not have gone any better," I said.

The same could not be said about my diagnostic acumen, however. The techs quickly stained the bone marrow smears, and I immediately looked at them under the microscope. I really wanted to know what was causing Sid's problems. As I looked at the slides, I was puzzled.

I had the same challenge as the clinicians, Dr. Rickert and Dr. Bruno. Why was there a single abnormality, low platelets, in an otherwise healthy, relatively young patient? Sid didn't have any disease associated with low platelets; he didn't have any diseases at all. He wasn't taking any medicines to cause his platelets to go down. This mystery could only be solved by going to the source of the platelets, where they were made, the bone marrow, and looking at what was there.

Which I did, and by any criteria Sid's bone marrow looked terrible. The cells in the bone marrow looked bizarre, like something from another planet. Usually the blood-forming cells of the bone marrow start out as young cells and then mature into red blood cells, white blood cells, and platelets. This happens in an orderly, well-defined manner.

But that wasn't happening in Sid's bone marrow, which was a haphazard mishmash of young cells and abnormal cells, which weren't maturing at all. The cells weren't maturing into platelets; no wonder Sid had low platelets. So I had an explanation for Sid's low platelets.

But as I looked at the bone marrow, the mystery deepened. Amazingly the bone marrow cells were *not* maturing into red blood cells or white blood cells either. Yet Sid was not anemic, and he had normal counts of white blood cells in his peripheral blood. Sid was admitted with a low platelet count only. Every other lab test when he came in was normal. But that didn't correlate with what I was seeing on the bone marrow smears, which didn't make any sense.

Morphologically, what I was seeing in the bone marrow wasn't particularly unusual; it even had a name – myelodysplastic syndrome (MDS). But what I was seeing had never been described in this situation, for two reasons:

1. MDS was a disease of older patients, in their seventies, eighties, and nineties. I had never seen a case in someone younger than sixty. Sid was thirty-eight years old.

2. I had never seen MDS associated with low platelets only. MDS, to my knowledge, was associated with not only low platelets (which Sid had), but always with anemia and low white blood cell counts (which Sid did not have).

I was totally confused. I was seeing a disease that I had never seen before, never read about, and as far as I could tell, had never ever been discovered or described.

Before I left for the day, Dr. Aaron Rickert, the hematologist-oncologist, stopped by my office to find out what I had found out so far. He was a short intense man, with red hair and a short red beard.

No greeting. "What's your diagnosis on Sid Barksdale?" he asked.

"The only thing I've looked at so far are the bone marrow smears."

"What do you see?"

"Myelodysplastic syndrome."

That stopped him. I could see his computer brain trying to process that diagnosis. His reaction was the same as mine, if a little more crude. "Bullshit. He's too young for that."

"I know."

"I was expecting a drug reaction or idiopathic thrombocytopenic purpura or thrombotic thrombocytopenic purpura…something along those lines."

"Yeah, so was I. He doesn't have any of that."

"Then what does he have? And don't tell me MDS."

"I don't know. I still have tissue studies – clot section and biopsy to look at, and the special studies – flow cytometry and cytogenetics. Hopefully I will know more then."

"When will you get all that done?"

"A couple of days."

"So you'll call me when you know more?"

"Right."

"Uh…you do know who Sid Barksdale is?"

"Yeah, actually I've known him a long time, know him pretty well."

"Then you know that he is a prominent member of the community."

"Yes, I know that Sid Barksdale is a prominent member of the community."

"I need a diagnosis, hopefully something I can treat, even cure. I mean, I can treat the MDS with platelet transfusions, but there is nothing I can do for him that is going to cure him or make him better."

"I know."

"Well, then you know that if we're missing something, something curable or treatable, well…"

"The consequences would be catastrophic."

"Right."

"I know."

I didn't tell Aaron this, but I really doubted that I would learn anything helpful after examining the rest of the bone marrow studies and results. I told him that stuff to get some uninterrupted time – time that I could use to do some reading, research, and reflection to figure out what was wrong with Sid.

It was late afternoon, and it had been a long day. I dissected the few remaining specimens I had to examine – a gallbladder and an appendix – and went home.

I was on another one of my diets, this time a vegetarian diet, so I had potatoes and creamed green beans, my own special recipe. I just had a few helpings. I also had some fresh peaches. My two boys had steak and potatoes. Sarah, my wife, had a salad.

After dinner I read the *Siegeburg Post*, our small-town newspaper. There was nothing in it about Sid Barksdale, thank God. Then Sarah and I sat out on our second-story deck overlooking the untamed wilderness otherwise known as our backyard. The name "untamed wilderness" was used by me and our neighbors because of the many trees and my less than compulsive landscaping. The August days in Siegeburg were hot, but the evenings were comfortable, especially for me because I like warm weather. Two squirrels put on the same show for us every evening. While it was still light out, they had dinner in the black walnut tree directly behind our deck, scurrying around and feasting on the walnuts. While they did that, I feasted on fresh cherries. Then at exactly 7:45 p.m. the squirrels finished eating, and each squirrel, one after the other, took a long leap from the walnut tree to an adjacent leafy elm, always leaving from the same oak tree branch, and landing on the same elm tree branch, like acrobats putting on a show. Once the squirrels were in the elm tree, they settled in for the night. Their performance ended each evening on a high note. I almost relaxed.

Sarah and I came in the house, and I turned on the TV. I channel surfed for a while and then went to bed around 9:30 p.m. After a little while I fell asleep and dreamed I was looking at bone marrow slides and couldn't figure out what was wrong, and everyone was watching.

When I got to my office the next morning, I sat down and waited for a flash of inspiration that would solve the mystery of Sid's disease. Didn't happen. So I pulled out some textbooks and read up on MDS. I also had a large collection of index cards with my notes on the various scientific/medical articles that I've read. I pulled out all the cards filed under myelodysplastic syndrome and read them. These were signs of desperation.

The information I reviewed just confirmed what I already knew: MDS occurred in old people. For it to occur in a thirty-eight-year-old man, like Sid, was unheard of and unreported. I looked at the bone marrow smears again; it was still MDS. I was missing something, something important.

I had a break until my morning slides would be ready to look at, including the slides from Sid's bone marrow clot section and biopsy. I used the waiting time to go see how Sid was doing, the day after the bone marrow collection procedure.

When I walked into his room, Sid was about to receive a platelet transfusion. The bag of platelets was quite pleasing to look at – a clear, flexible plastic bottle containing a lifesaving amber elixir. I noted with approval that the two nurses double-checked Sid's name verbally, as well as checking his armband to make sure everything matched up. When that was completed, they hung the platelets on a pole and hooked them to his IV line. I waited for them to leave and then checked the bone marrow wound site. I peeled off the four-by-four sponges and looked at the wound, which looked great – no swelling, no bleeding – you could barely tell anything had happened. I put a couple of sterile four-by-four sponges on the wound and covered everything with tape.

"Do you know what's wrong with me?" asked Sid.

"Yes…and no."

"What does that mean?"

"I think you have myelodysplastic syndrome."

"That sounds pretty bad."

I wasn't jealous of Sid anymore. I felt kind of silly, really, about how the past bothered me, made me envious, bitter. But I didn't want to get into that with Sid. Not the time or the place. Probably never would be the time or place.

I simply said, "It is. But I'm puzzled. I've never seen this disease in someone as young as you – never even heard of it. Also, I've never seen this disease with low platelets only – everything else normal."

I nodded at the platelet transfusion. "The only thing you need is platelets. You don't need transfusions of red blood cells, white blood cells, plasma...nothing else, just platelets. I've never seen anything like it. No one has."

"Could something have caused it?"

"Sure. Let's go through the list. Have you been around any radiation?"

"No."

"Been around insecticides, pesticides?"

"No, I'm a city boy."

"Worked with any chemicals, say benzene?"

"No. I hated science, you know that. Unlike you, who loved that stuff."

I shook my head. "Yeah, I figured as much. Obviously you're not on any chemotherapy, for cancer or anything?"

"Right."

"Are you on any medicines at all?"

"No. Just a one-a-day vitamin. I'm in good health."

I paused. I don't like interacting with patients. That's why I became a pathologist. I like disease, patients not so much. Finally I said, "You don't check any of the boxes. I don't know why I'm seeing what I am seeing in your bone marrow."

Sid pondered that. Then he said, "I think you will, eventually."

The nurse came in to check that the platelet transfusion was proceeding smoothly, with no transfusion reaction. She checked Sid's blood pressure and pulse, which were normal. She asked if Sid was feeling okay, any chest discomfort, difficulty breathing, or pain anywhere.

"I'm feeling fine," said Sid.

The nurse left the room.

I said, "Right now I don't have all the answers. I've got some more slides coming out today, and some tests are pending. Hopefully that additional data will help."

"I think you will figure out what's wrong with me. Thank you, Jack."

As I walked back to my office, I pondered Sid's comments and his confidence in me. I was not confident. I was scared.

Later that morning the bone marrow clot section and biopsy slides were ready to examine, and the results of the special studies were back. I looked at the slides and reviewed the data from the special studies. They were no real help, but just confirmed what I already knew: Sid had MDS, but there was no explanation for this occurring in someone so young presenting with low platelets only, nothing else wrong.

As a pathologist, the only thing I have to offer to patients and their doctors, to anyone…is diagnoses, i.e., answers. I don't dispense medicines, sew up wounds, do appendectomies, perform heart transplants…none of that stuff. Just look at specimens and make interpretations and diagnoses. That's it.

But that's a lot. The stakes here were enormous. A diagnosis of MDS was a death sentence. There was no cure and really no effective treatment. In Sid's case, the only helpful thing to do was give platelet transfusions, but that was a losing battle. As soon as the platelets were transfused, they were used up, because Sid's bone marrow was not making any platelets at all. It was like trying to keep a pail filled with water or milk or cider, and the pail has a hole in the bottom. Eventually you can't keep up, and the pail goes dry.

It was me against the disease, or at least the diagnosis of a disease, and the outcome was in doubt, a toss-up. I was bothered by this, bothered a lot.

Dr. Aaron Rickert was unsympathetic when he came into my office that afternoon. He dealt every day with patients who were dying of cancer. Now *they* had problems. A pathologist struggling to make a diagnosis? That wasn't a problem, that was his job.

"I need a diagnosis," said Aaron.

"MDS," I said.

"Can you give me a little more to go on?"

"No. That's all I got."

"Well, I want more, I need more, I gots to have more."

"Do you want to look at the slides?" I asked.

He did. We went out to the lab, where there was a teaching micro-scope, so both of us could see the same thing under the microscope – an optical connection. I pointed out the features of MDS and why I thought MDS was the correct diagnosis. Then we talked about the things that didn't fit.

I said, "You are an experienced clinician. Can you think of anything that would explain why a patient so young would have MDS, manifest-ing as low platelets only?"

Aaron thought for ten to fifteen seconds. "No."

We rehashed Sid's medical history, findings…everything, but didn't make any progress in making a definitive diagnosis. The thing was though, making a definitive diagnosis wasn't Aaron's job. His job was to treat the patient. Making a definitive diagnosis, that was *my* job.

I needed help. As you read this book, it may seem to you that I sure need a lot of help, that I'm not all that smart and not a particularly strong person, and that I'm kind of insecure. That assessment is correct.

However, let me point out two things:

1. If I told stories about the specimens and patients who had straightforward diagnoses, well, there's not much drama, con-flict, or suspense in that, and my considered opinion is that you would be bored and stop reading. I regard that as catastrophic.

2. I wish I *were* smarter and more heroic. I also wish I were better looking. I do the best with what I have. I believe I am a good thinker, but not a genius. I have encountered very few geniuses in my lifetime, and right now I can only think of three. The first one was Arthur Ashe, when I watched him play tennis, in per-son. He made tennis look easy. The second genius was Nolan Ryan, who made throwing strikes at ninety-five miles an hour look easy. The third genius was Dr. Bruce Callister, the man I

was going to call, my mentor during med school and residency. He was a genius at what he did, although he didn't always make it look easy. In fact, he wasn't always right. Still, he was the smartest man I ever encountered.

Dr. Callister was still on the pathology faculty at Ivory. I phoned him and asked if I could get his help on a case. He said he was really tied up for the rest of the day – the next several days actually, but that I could meet him in his office at 10 p.m. I said I'd be there.

That evening I drove from Siegeburg to Ivory Medical Center. I knew Dr. Callister would be punctual, so I arrived fifteen minutes early. The corridor where his office was located was quiet; all the offices were closed and locked up. I waited in the hallway. There was minimal lighting. While I waited, I looked at the pictures of previous pathology house staff that lined the walls. The picture from 1978 included Dr. Callister and me.

Dr. Callister arrived at exactly 10 p.m. He nodded at me, didn't say anything. I nodded back. He unlocked his office, and we went in. It hadn't changed since I was a medical student – same fish tank in the outer reception area, same inner office filled with books and a teaching microscope. Dr. Callister hadn't changed much either – same sturdy build and crew cut. He sat down at the microscope, and I sat across from him.

"Watcha got?" he asked.

I handed over the folders with the thirty-two microscopic slides of the case, as well as a cover letter with the clinical information about Sid – the history, physical findings – everything I knew about the case. Dr. Callister looked it over, asked me a few questions for clarification, and then started looking at the microscopic slides. I looked on with him, seeing the same thing he did. It brought back memories of my pathology residency. I was still learning.

Dr. Callister looked at the slides one by one, rapidly but thoroughly. Every so often he stopped to look up something in the paperwork or to ask me a question.

After about twenty-five minutes, he was done. He pushed his chair back from the microscope and started rubbing his chin, his "tell" that this was a tough case.

"I think you are on the right track," he said. "This patient clearly has MDS."

"Right," I said.

"You are probably wondering why this disease is in someone so young, and why the low platelets, everything else normal."

"Right."

Dr. Callister shuffled through the paperwork. "I didn't see an arsenic level," he said. "You know arsenic poisoning can cause these kinds of changes in the bone marrow, with death. Some experts think Napoleon Bonaparte died of arsenic poisoning."

"It came back today, late, after I dictated the cover letter. It was negative."

"Okay."

He pondered a while, lost in thought. Then he got up and walked to one of his many file cabinets filled with index cards summarizing his reading. He found what he wanted and brought the cards back to his microscope and perused them. Neither one of us said anything for a few minutes.

"You know, Jack, we look for patterns in what we do know, to see if we can apply them to what we don't know."

"I agree. So what's your thinking?"

"We'll get there. You of course are familiar with Kaposi's sarcoma?"

"Yes."

"When you trained here, how often did you make the diagnosis of Kaposi's sarcoma?"

"Once, in the whole four years I was here."

"How old was the patient?"

"Ninety-one."

"In your practice now, how often do you make the diagnosis of Kaposi's sarcoma?"

"Three times a week."

"How old are the patients?"

"They are young men, with AIDS."

Dr. Callister nodded, then said, "How about *Pneumocystis* pneumonia, how often did you see that when you were here?"

"Almost never."

"How often do you see it now?"

"Almost every day, in patients who have AIDS."

Dr. Callister nodded again. "Do you see a pattern here?"

It was late, and it had been a long day, but Dr. Callister wanted me to figure this out myself.

So I did. "So you think my patient, Sid Barksdale, has AIDS."

Dr. Callister shrugged. "I think so," he said.

"I've done a lot of work on this case and haven't seen anything that describes MDS in AIDS. Do you have any data – some literature to back that up?"

Dr. Callister handed one of his index cards to me. It summarized an obscure journal that I'd never heard of – *Case Reports in Hematology*. As I read it, Dr. Callister talked: "It's rare, but MDS has been reported in patients with AIDS. That article says 0.3% of AIDS patients had MDS."

I said, "0.3%, that's a pretty small number. Maybe it was just coincidence."

"Maybe. But interestingly, in that 0.3%, MDS was the first symptom of the HIV infection, which is exactly what happened to your patient. And none of those patients knew they had AIDS, just like your patient."

I continued to think. I was overwhelmed. Sid Barksdale, my friend, happily married with two kids, a prominent member of the community…had AIDS. I remembered a few years earlier when patients about my age (young), who were male and unmarried, presented with weight loss, fever, and anemia, so they had bone marrow studies, which were not diagnostic of anything. And for quite some time we couldn't figure out what was wrong with them as they got sicker and sicker, because the disease they had hadn't been discovered yet. After a year or two, after medical reports from the Center for Disease Control and other medical centers, we made the correct diagnosis. They had AIDS. But we were still learning.

I focused back to the present and replied to Dr. Callister. "Just like my patient," I repeated. "Young and healthy except for MDS."

"And AIDS."

I looked at the index card again, front and back. "But my patient is different," I said. "Sid Barksdale just has low platelets. These patients were typical MDS patients – they were also anemic, with low white blood cell counts. That's the other unique feature of this patient's disease, low platelets, everything else normal."

Neither one of us said anything for a minute or two. We were thinking. Even Dr. Callister was kind of stumped. Then he said, "With AIDS, so many things have been unique, a new disease if you will, out of nowhere, really. What I am struck with, about the disease, is that things that happen in this disease are the same, but different somehow. Kaposi's sarcoma is still Kaposi's sarcoma, but it looks a little different than the Kaposi's sarcoma we used to see – you agree?"

"Yes."

"Same thing with *Pneumocystis* infection."

"Agree."

"I think MDS will be similar, same disease process, but different, somehow, in this case, with low platelets, everything else normal, at least initially."

I said, "You know who this is, don't you, this patient, Sid Barksdale, a pillar of the community, banker, state representative…"

"I know who he is."

"Husband, father of two girls, churchgoer…He has no risk factors for AIDS – he's not gay, he doesn't use IV drugs, never had a blood transfusion, doesn't have hemophilia, so he doesn't get blood products…I can't believe he has AIDS."

"Jack, you don't know if he has AIDS or not. I don't either. You have to do the tests – HIV antibody and, if that's positive, a Western blot."

"Okay. But I know Sid Barksdale, known him for a long time. I can't believe he has AIDS."

"How well does anyone know another person?"

I thought about Dr. Callister's comments on my drive back to Siegeburg. It was late, almost midnight, little traffic. I was focused on the road, but the rest of my mind was empty and receptive. I do some of my best thinking while driving, with the radio off, just me, the car, and the road. As I am driving, the solution to a problem I am working on, seeming insoluble, will come out of…somewhere. I realized that Dr. Callister's comments had the "ring of truth." Also, as Sherlock Holmes said, "Once you eliminate the impossible, whatever remains, no matter how improbable, must be the truth."

Sid Barksdale had MDS and AIDS.

I didn't sleep much. The next morning I was at the hospital at 6 a.m. Whether I wanted to be or not, years in medicine had bludgeoned me into a morning person. So many things at a hospital occur in the morning – rounds, surgery, meetings, phone calls, emergencies…if you go into medicine, you'd better be a morning person or become one.

I was dreading my conversation with Sid, so I wanted to get it over with as soon as possible. I got settled in my office, checked a few things, and then walked to his room.

Sid was awake, sitting up in his bed, reading the *Siegeburg Post*. A bag of normal saline was running into the IV line inserted in the back of his left wrist. We had the room to ourselves.

Sid smiled at me. "What's going on?" he said.

"I'm in kind of an awkward situation."

"I have AIDS, right?"

That stopped me. "How did you know that?" I asked.

"The look on your face. I'm a politician, remember. That's what I'm good at, reading people. And I know about my risk factors. You didn't."

"What risk factors?"

"I've always loved beauty, in women, sure, but also men. I probably should have been more careful in whom I loved, taken more precautions, but then at the time…who knew?"

Sid took a deep breath and sighed.

I continued. "At this point, nothing is definite. We can do the tests to confirm the diagnosis. We should do the tests. In fact, we *have* to do the tests."

"Okay."

"Right. I'll get started, then. See you later, my friend." I had nothing left. It was time for me to leave.

Sid motioned me to hold up. "Before you go, I want to tell you something."

I waited.

"Thank you for helping me, taking care of me," he said.

"Of course. But no need to do that. I mean, it's my job. That's what I do."

"You know, I've always envied you, even been a little afraid of you."

If someone told me I had extraterrestrial parents, I would not have been more surprised. Are you kidding me?

Trying to control my emotions, I said, "I envied *you.*"

Sid chuckled and said, "You were so smart, you *are* so smart – always knew what you wanted to do – be a doctor – and then did it. Most people don't know what they want, don't know what they're supposed to do, and they struggle. You're lucky."

I couldn't talk anymore, so I left.

Two days later Sid's test results came back. His HIV antibody test was positive, and so was the Western blot. I made the diagnosis: Sid had MDS secondary to AIDS. It was a death sentence.

Sid was still in the hospital. He would be discharged later that day. I owed it to him to deliver the news myself, so I did. He was still in his hospital gown, but the IV was out, and he had khaki pants and a golf shirt laid out, ready to wear. I told him why he was sick.

"I figured the plague would get me sooner or later," he said. "I don't want anyone else to know. Can you keep it confidential?"

"Sure. The test results are still in the lab; they're not in the medical chart, which is the way it will stay. Obviously Dr. Rickert has the results, and he'll discuss treatment options with you. It's an infectious disease that gets reported to the State Health Department. Who else finds out is up to you and Dr. Rickert. Carole needs to know so she can get tested. But, yeah, from our end in the lab, we can keep everything confidential."

"Maybe I'll change my mind, but for now I want to keep my diagnosis a secret."

"It's your call."

Sid was silent but restless for about half a minute. I didn't rush anything. Then he said, "I dunno, maybe people should find out about this plague that I have it, so that they can take precautions, something I didn't do until it was too late."

I kind of shrugged. I had nothing to add. I was Sid's doctor, a pathologist – not his moral guide. Can anyone be a moral guide for

someone else? Maybe a few, but I'm not one of them. I had always per-
ceived Sid as one such person.

Sid continued, "You know, it's hard to live a secret life; it takes a lot
of energy. I'm really tired."

"I can understand that."

"Really, Jack? Do you know what it feels like to pretend that you
have it all together, that you have all the answers, like otherwise people
wouldn't like you or love you? The time and energy it takes to be the
best – the best law student, best businessman, best politician, the best
husband, best father, best…everything. Do you, Jack, do you know?"

"Yeah."

I phoned Dr. Callister with the follow-up, that Sid did turn out to
have AIDS. Of course, that's what he had expected.

I said, "This needs to be published – the first case of HIV infection
with initial symptoms of low platelets caused by myelodysplastic syndrome. It's never been described."

"Then publish it," said Dr. Callister.

"You want to be co-author, help me write it?"

"No."

"No? This is important!"

"The answer is no. You're the guy who wants to be a writer. Write."
He hung up.

That's what I did, all by myself. I wrote up Sid's illness as a case
report and submitted it to the *Archives of Pathology and Laboratory
Medicine.* In the acceptance letter the editor of the publication said of
my findings: "This case report advances our scientific knowledge of
AIDS slightly and perhaps significantly." It was the first time my name
was in print. I was a writer.

Sid wasn't in the hospital much over the next few years. He got most
of his care as an outpatient. I rarely saw him. A few times he stopped by
to see me in my office when he came to the lab to get his blood drawn
for some follow-up tests. Sid was pleasant to me, and I was pleasant to
him, but we really didn't have much to say to each other. We just had
matter-of-fact discussions about his disease.

Sid kept his diagnosis a secret. His wife, Carole, was told, but no one else. Her tests were negative, and she stayed in good health. She continued to work as a nurse in the endoscopy suite at the hospital. I saw Carole more than I saw Sid. From her demeanor no one could discern that she was about to be a widow.

Carole stayed in the marriage. Sid and Carole were kept busy raising their two daughters, Kim and Carey, who were told their father was sick, nothing more.

From what I could tell, everyone else was told even less. Sid finished up his two-year term as state representative and did not run for re-election. He retired from politics. Sid pretty much retired from life. He was obviously sick and didn't get out in the community much.

Most people don't know what a pathologist does other than "do autopsies." Actually I rarely did autopsies, and over 99% of my time was spent taking care of living patients. Few in Siegeburg knew that. Therefore I was privy to conversations about patients that I took care of – conversations that would not have taken place in front of another kind of doctor, say a surgeon or family practitioner. I was regarded as just a doctor in the laboratory who "doesn't take care of patients."

So often I felt like the Shadow as I listened to people in the community talk about patients who had been diagnosed and treated at Excel McClain Hospital. I never said a word.

About Sid, I never heard a hint of scandal. Everyone who knew Sid knew he was sick. It was obvious. He lost a lot of weight, and there were many days he didn't feel good. In fact, he felt awful. But no one knew he had AIDS. The explanations I did hear for his illness were novel and creative.

For example, I attended my youngest son's Junior Pro basketball game and sat next to another parent. He knew Sid and talked to me about how sad it was that Sid had picked up that parasite in Brazil. The basis for this story was that right before he got sick, Sid went on a political mission to Siegeburg's sister city, Flores, Brazil, near Manaus, in the Amazon jungle region. While he was there Sid supposedly picked up some sort of lethal untreatable jungle parasite that was going to kill him. "They just can't seem to cure it," said the parent.

Another explanation I heard when I attended a production of *Brigadoon* by McClain Christian Academy. Again I was seated next to a parent who knew Sid, and knew that Sid was "dying of lung cancer," which wasn't fair in this man's opinion, because "Sid never smoked."

I listened but didn't say a word.

One year after the start of his symptoms, I read Sid's obituary in the *Siegeburg Post.* It was several paragraphs long and emphasized his public service and said he died quietly at home after a long illness.

DISCIPLINE

August 1990

"I'm a hunter not a farmer," said Dr. Morris Benson.

This was said at a meeting of the Executive Committee of Excel McClain Hospital. It was actually more of a hearing and an appeal – a specially called meeting to address a problem.

The problem was Dr. Morris Benson.

The setting was simple. A large multipurpose room with light blue carpet was partitioned by floor-to-ceiling dividers to make a smaller room, to fit the number of attendees, which only numbered around a dozen. That small space was largely filled by three rectangular folding tables, with gray metal work and white tops. They were pushed together to form a U. There was only one door to enter or leave this partitioned area, which was brightly lit with overhead fluorescent lights. The members seated themselves on the outside of the U. Dr. Morris Benson was seated in the open space of the U, like a witness. In front of each committee member was a three-ring binder with a black cover, filled with documents.

The Executive Committee is the only hospital committee of real importance. The various other committees – infection control, blood and tissue, pharmacy, critical care – are pretty much a waste of time – reviewing a lot of statistics and rubber-stamping policies and procedures already written. The meetings are pro forma and boring.

The Executive Committee meetings are not necessarily pro forma or boring. In fact, they can be quite interesting if conflict is your thing.

The Executive Committee was made up of the chairs of the various departments, and the chief of the medical staff.

Dr. Steve Prescott represented the Internal Medicine Department. He was in his early forties. He was recruited by Dr. Bob, but then went out into practice on his own. He took his calling as a physician very seriously. He was a zealot.

Dr. Diane Murtaugh represented pediatrics. She was forty-one years old. She was quite attractive, but never married. She regarded the patients in her pediatric practice as her children. Not only did she take care of their health, but she monitored their grades in school, handing out prizes for good grades. Her attic was filled with toys, teddy bears, and other presents that she handed out for various achievements by her patients. She had just been named the Physician of the Year in Tennessee, quite an honor.

Dr. Rob Masterson represented the ob-gyn department. He was a short little guy, with blond hair. He was creative, liked to write poems. He was bipolar, well controlled with lithium.

Dr. Mitch Thornburg represented the surgery department. He was in his late fifties. He had long white hair and was a big bear of a man. He looked like a crazy person. He worked almost all the time, either doing surgery or seeing patients in his office. He brought millions of dollars in revenue each month into Excel McClain Hospital.

John Tindale represented anesthesiology. He was in his mid-thirties. He was a tall, lanky, slim, pleasant-appearing man with the kind of soothing demeanor that you want around the operating room.

David Reynolds represented radiology. He was in his mid-fifties. He had a lean gray wolf-like appearance. He was very smart and very political.

Jack Spenser represented pathology. He was forty-one years old. He was a short little guy. He was a hospital-based physician, one of the RAPERS (*R*adiologists, *A*nesthesiologists, *P*athologists, *ER* docs). The derogatory nickname came from the fact that these specialists didn't generate their own patients, but had practices based on referrals from primary care doctors – internists, pediatricians, surgeons, and other clinicians.

Frank Moneypenny represented the emergency room docs. He was an angular guy with long arms and long legs. He was in his late thirties.

Dr. Tom Bruno represented orthopedics. He had light gray hair, almost white. He was slim, average height and weight, but very muscular and wiry. He used to play football as a safety for the United States Military Academy at West Point. When he finished his military service, he went to medical school and then trained as an orthopedic surgeon at Massachusetts General Hospital. He was fifty-six years old.

Dr. Aaron Rickert, an oncologist, was the chief of the medical staff. He went to college at the Massachusetts Institute of Technology (MIT). He went to med school at Harvard. He did his internal medicine rotation and oncology training at Washington University Hospital in St. Louis. He was in his early thirties.

Ex-officio members were Bryan Magnuson, CEO of the hospital, and Kathy Lassiter, chief operating officer (COO) of the hospital. They were sitting next to each other as usual. They were always together, with Bryan looking to Kathy for guidance. Bryan went to college at Duke, which he never let you forget. Kathy went to Tennessee Tech in Cookeville, and she didn't care if you forgot that or not. Both were in their mid-thirties.

Another ex-officio member was Annie Layne, the operating room director. She wore maroon scrubs covered by a white lab coat. As usual her hair was covered by a green surgical cap, which all the guys in the room regretted, because she was a quite attractive brunette. She was in her early thirties and relatively new to the job. She had recently replaced Mary Ellen Masters, who had retired after twenty-seven years on the job.

The other person in the room was the problem, Dr. Morris Benson, a gastroenterologist, forty-one years old. He was a big man, not fat, not overly muscular like one of those bodybuilding types, but just a big guy, a little over six feet tall. His face seemed top heavy because the most prominent part of his face was his forehead, which seemed to take up his whole face. Of course, that is anatomically impossible, so in reality his forehead was probably about half his face, but that's no exaggeration. It was huge. His nose was sizeable as well, but he had a relatively small mouth and thin lips. He had light gray hair, even though he was only in his early forties. He was a good doctor, well educated and well trained. He had gone to medical school at the University of Kansas. He had done his internal medicine training and gastroenterology subspecialty training at Baylor Medical Center in Houston, Texas. He knew his stuff.

All that notwithstanding, the problem Dr. Benson presented to the Executive Committee was this: What do you do when you have a physician who is talented, smart, takes good care of patients, but is a *total asshole*? What *do* you do?

"I'm a hunter not a farmer," Dr. Benson repeated. "I don't think that this committee took that into account when you recommended that I be suspended from the medical staff for three weeks and put on probation for three years. I think that's excessive. I think it's indefensible. In fact, I think any punishment whatsoever is excessive…"

"How so?" interrupted Steve Prescott, the internist.

As Dr. Benson addressed the committee, he sat straight up, so that the effect was that he seemed bigger than he really was. "If I could continue with my opening statement…?"

Aaron Rickert, the oncologist and chairman, said, "Before we go any further, I would like to point out that this is the first step in the appeal process as outlined in the bylaws. This is an informal part of the process, without the presence of attorneys for either side. The purpose of this meeting is that Dr. Benson can be heard, and that we can answer any questions that need to be addressed. Please continue, Dr. Benson."

"Throughout history the five percent of us who are productive, who do the work of the world, who are the movers and shakers, have been hounded and harassed. I've single-handedly kept the Gastroenterology Service going, in spite of its problems and the problems in the operating room, and this is the thanks I get!"

Dr. Benson stopped talking. There was silence for a few beats.

Aaron Rickert said, "So that concludes your statement?"

"Yes. I would be happy to answer any questions."

"Thank you, Dr. Benson," said Dr. Rickert.

"What are the problems in the operating room that you perceive?" asked Dr. Thornberg, the general surgeon.

"We're short-staffed. The people in the operating room are losers. The OR schedule is a joke. The cases start late and run late."

"We're short-staffed because of you," said Kathy Lassiter, the COO. "You've run off a lot of people." Annie Layne, the OR director, nodded in agreement.

"They were losers," said Dr. Benson.

Kathy said, "We haven't been able to replace them because you are known throughout the medical community for your temper tantrums, the way you demean people, your outbursts, and your generally disruptive behavior."

Bryan Magnuson smiled at Kathy in an encouraging manner.

John Tindale, the anesthesiologist, said, "The problem with scheduling is *you,* Dr. Benson. You are often late for your cases. Under your direction we put patients to sleep, ready for their procedures. Then you disappear. We don't know where you go. You're not in your office, because we phone your office, and whoever answers says you aren't there. We beep you, and you don't answer. We don't know where you go, or what you do. We don't know if you are dealing with your personal problems or what, but we can't find you, and when you finally show up, you're late for your case, which puts *everyone* behind. Then, thanks to you, the whole OR schedule is messed up, and you blame everyone but yourself."

Dr. Benson closed his eyes and gathered himself. "None of you know what it is like to operate like I do – work fast, work well. No one else can do twelve cases a day, keep going, not make a mistake, and not miss anything. Nobody. I position that colonoscope perfectly, and I can see that it is exactly where it's supposed to be. Then I twist it just right, advance it perfectly, and inspect carefully as I go along. I don't miss anything. When I do an esophago/gastro/duodenoscopy, same thing. No one does it better. No one does it as well. No one. I'm focused, and everything else, like all this bullshit, is irrelevant."

Kathy Lassiter said, "Your two ex-partners are afraid of you and what you might do to them or their families."

"That's preposterous! I'm not a threat to anyone. I just want this over with so I can get back to my practice. I don't give a hoot about my ex-partners. Look, I'll admit that this has been a rough year. I brought in two gastroenterologists to be part of my growing practice. They were straight out of their residencies – didn't know anything about the real world of private practice. I vouched for them, helped get them privileges to work at this hospital, got them started, with a waiting list of patients ready for them to see – which is a heck of a lot more help than I got when I started here. Then, instead of being grateful, they stabbed me in the back. They moved out, in the middle of the night, and opened their own office in the same building! But that's okay, it's a free country – although I might point out that they violated the non-compete clauses in their contracts. But I let it go. I let it go – because we have to practice together, at this hospital, in the same department, use the same operating rooms…so I try to get along with them. But we have to communicate about scheduling cases and covering the emergency room and other issues – but they won't talk to me!"

Kathy Lassiter said, "That could be because of what happened in the dictation room."

Dr. Benson looked truly puzzled. "I don't know what you are talking about."

"Dr. Susan Owens, your ex-partner, says that you physically blocked the exit from the room when she tried to leave, and that you grabbed her by the arm and threatened her – said, 'I know where you live.' We can't have that kind of stuff here, we just can't. This is a hospital."

Dr. Benson shook his head in disbelief. "That's totally false. What happened is this: I said to Susan, 'You know it would be better for all concerned if we could at least talk to each other.' But it was like she didn't even hear me, didn't even know I was there. So I tapped her on the arm to get her attention. I didn't 'grab her' or threaten her or keep her from leaving. No way."

Kathy Lassiter said, "Believe me, your former partners are not vindictive. They just want to get on with their lives."

Dr. Rob Masterson, the ob-gyn, said, "As you know, I tried to step in and improve relations between you and the operating room staff." He nodded in the direction of Annie Layne, the OR director. "But the meeting I set up to do that lasted only fifteen minutes before you lost it and called Miss Layne a…" He nodded again in the direction of Annie. "Well, I'm not going to repeat it here."

Annie Layne hunched her shoulders slightly. She did not like being the center of attention, at all.

Dr. Masterson continued, "That's not the way to address a co-worker. That's not the way to address anyone. That was totally unprofessional."

Dr. Benson said, "I meant to say 'witch,' because she directs a coven of witches."

"That's also unprofessional," said Dr. Masterson.

"What's unprofessional is for her and her staff to talk about me behind my back. For a long time I haven't responded to what's been said about me. I just took care of my patients. But eventually I couldn't stay silent anymore. I'm a pretty upfront guy. I guess I lost it that one time at that meeting. But it was just that one time."

Annie Layne shook her head gently from side to side. Her voice quavered. She said, "That actually happens all the time. But this was the first time you got caught. Usually you are too clever to do something like that around somebody who matters."

An uneasy silence entered the room. Physicians as a general rule do not like conflict. They tend to be healers, not fighters. The members of the Executive Committee restlessly looked through the documents in the binders in front of them, or they looked around, waiting for some leadership. Dr. Benson's gaze went from person to person, looking directly at each one intensely, a nonverbal challenge. Bryan Magnuson looked away. Kathy Lassiter, Anna Layne, and the members of the committee just stared back at Dr. Benson and said nothing.

Finally, Dr. Rickert, the oncologist and chairman of the committee, said, "Why did you break off contact with Dr. Todd?"

Dr. Benson was briefly confused and said, "Dr. Todd?" Then he said, "Oh yeah, the guy from the state, the guy from the Impaired Physicians Program?"

"Correct. You were clearly instructed by this committee to seek the help of Dr. Todd and his program."

"Right. I broke off contact with him because I'm not impaired. It's just that I'm a hunter surrounded by a bunch of farmers. Besides, I didn't break off contact with him. *He* broke off contact with *me.* But that's okay. I don't need him. I keep my own counsel."

Dr. Rickert took a document out of the three-ring binder in front of him. He glanced at the document and then took it over to Dr. Benson. Dr. Rickert said, "This is a copy of a letter, which I am sure you've seen, from Dr. Todd, addressed to you and me. In it he says that you broke off communications with him. He also describes your incredible lack of insight into your problems, and your refusal to take ownership of them or take any responsibility whatsoever for them. Again, you were clearly told by the Impaired Physicians Committee of this hospital to seek the advocacy of Dr. Todd's organization to keep your medical staff privileges, and you didn't do it."

"It was a conspiracy to make me do that, totally out of line. Besides, I *have* seen him. I saw him last Monday."

Kathy Lassiter, the COO, said, "But you only did that after this committee took action to suspend you immediately. Clearly the only reason you re-established contact was to improve your chances of succeeding with this appeal."

"Doesn't look like it did much good," said Dr. Benson.

David Reynolds, the radiologist, said, "I think we all need to remember that Dr. Benson has been an active member of this medical staff for a long time, something like fifteen or twenty years, and has been an important part of this hospital's success. He was fine, never had any problems until he started having those tragedies in his personal life that we all know about."

"That has nothing to do with anything," said Dr. Benson.

Dr. Murtaugh, the pediatrician, said, "Look, Morris, we took this action for your sake as well the sake of the hospital. You need help. We should have done something like this years ago. I just hope it's not too late for you."

"The times I was out of control were in the spring, when I had to take steroids for my asthma, prescribed by my pulmonologist."

Kathy Lassiter said, "That used to be true. It used to be that things would go along fine, even for years. But then there would be some kind of eruption, which tends to happen in the spring, when once again you would be out of control. But lately the intervals between outbursts have gotten shorter, and the episodes of your disruptive behavior have gotten longer."

"I'm not believing this," said Dr. Benson. "I guess when you're better than anyone else, you're a target and people come after you. I'm a victim of backstabbing and innuendo, which is not the way I handle things. If I have a problem with people, I address them directly."

Dr. Tindale, the anesthesiologist, said, "Actually, that's not possible. You've disrupted every meeting we set up to do that. The operating room staff is afraid to speak up; they're terrified you'll retaliate against them. I've lost track of how many OR nurses you've run off."

Dr. Benson shook his head gently, took in a deep sigh, and let it out. No one said anything for a few beats.

Aaron Rickert, oncologist and chair of the committee, said, "I think it's time to wrap this up. Before we excuse Dr. Benson, is there anything anyone wants to add?"

Dr. Tom Bruno, the orthopedic surgeon, said, "I, for one, am sick of giving breaks to this jerk."

Dr. Rickert said, "Thank you for your input, Dr. Bruno. Dr. Benson, you are excused."

After Dr. Benson left, Dr. Rickert said, "You know, this hunter versus farmer stuff really isn't relevant. I mean, everyone in this room is an aggressive type A personality. That doesn't justify Dr. Benson's behavior."

There was no other discussion. The Executive Committee voted unanimously to proceed with the three-month suspension and three-year probation, which would commence at the close of business that day.

"What's the next step?" asked Dr. Spenser, the pathologist.

Kathy Lassiter pulled out her copy of the bylaws, a thick book with a black binder, opened it to the applicable place, and paraphrased what it said. Dr. Benson had two options:

1. He could formally appeal the penalties, with his attorney present if he wished, and try to get the decisions reversed.
2. He could accept the ruling of the Executive Committee, which would be passed on to the Board of Trust of the Hospital. The board would certainly accept the decision of the Executive Committee.

As chairman, Dr. Rickert was tasked with relating the news to Dr. Benson by phone or in person. A formal letter would follow.

After the meeting Dr. Rickert went to his office. He dreaded the conversation with Dr. Benson, so he phoned Dr. Benson as soon as he got there. Dr. Rickert wanted this *over with*. He phoned the operating room suite, hoping to catch Dr. Benson either between cases or before he got started. When Dr. Benson came to the phone, Dr. Rickert told him the decision of the Executive Committee. Dr. Rickert continued, "You can finish out the day, do the operations you have scheduled, but then you need to postpone any work at this hospital for three weeks and arrange for someone else to take care of your patients during that time."

"Okay."

"You can read the bylaws to see your options at this point, but basically you can formally appeal your suspension and probation, or accept it."

"I'll think about it."

After his appearance at the Executive Committee meeting, Dr. Benson proceeded to do a day's work. He did eight endoscopy procedures. The procedures Dr. Benson did were appropriate, with good indications to do the procedures. The specimens that Dr. Benson sent to Dr. Spenser would have real pathology, something to treat. As usual Dr. Benson performed the operations flawlessly. There were no complications – no bleeding, no ruptured tissues, no perforations, and no reaction to the sedation…everything was perfect. And the tissue specimens he collected while he was there, the biopsies, were not only adequate, but they were generous. He made sure that Dr. Spenser would have plenty of tissue to examine, so Dr. Spenser could to *his* job and diagnose what was going on.

Thinking of Dr. Spenser, Dr. Benson decided to talk to him as soon as possible.

Which was midafternoon. Dr. Benson finished his cases in the operating room suite and walked across the hall to Jack Spenser's office. The door to Jack's office was closed. Dr. Benson knocked once and immediately walked in. Jack was looking through his AO 110 microscope, a stack of slide folders to his left and a stack of papers to his right. Dr. Benson had high regard for Dr. Spenser, mainly because he was one of the few doctors around who could talk about something besides medicine – like books, art, music, and sculpture. In fact, come to think of it, Jack was the *only* physician Morris Benson wanted to talk to about that stuff. Jack motioned Dr. Benson to sit down, which he did, the desk between him and Dr. Spenser. Dr. Spenser reached into his bookcase and handed over *Bonfire of the Vanities*, by Tom Wolfe.

"Great book," said Jack. "Thanks for loaning it to me."

"I thought you would like it," said Morris.

"It's about what happens when we regard those not like us as *the other*."

"Right."

"That lesson may be applicable to what happened this morning," said Jack.

"You didn't say much," said Morris.

"Wasn't much to say. I like dealing with specimens, people not so much. Politics not at all."

"Yeah. Me too. I like doing my job, not wasting my time defending myself."

"What are you going to do?"

"Defend myself. I've got a lawyer who is telling me to fight it."

Jack shook his head in disagreement. "You won't win. You are good at your job, not so good at politics. You have to let go of this Nietzsche 'Will to Power' stuff. In medicine that attitude won't get you very far."

"Why?"

"Society gives physicians a lot of privileges, literally life and death, so the system is very careful about who gets those privileges. Consequently, entities like the Executive Committee have a lot of power. You can fight, but you can't win. The Executive Committee can pretty much do whatever it wants to do – in the name of [Jack pantomimed air quotes] 'patient care.'"

"Are you telling me all this as a pathologist or a friend?"

"Both, but mainly I hate to see a great talent go to waste. You send me good specimens that are diagnostic. Some of your colleagues, who will go unnamed, are too timid and don't send me enough tissue. I have to sign them out as 'insufficient tissue available for diagnosis' or 'nondiagnostic' or something else not helpful – very frustrating. So I don't want you to lose your privileges."

"Sounds reasonable."

"Oh, don't get me wrong, another gastroenterologist would come along and take your place, but that person wouldn't be as good as you."

"You got *that* right."

Jack shrugged.

Morris said, "So I should just go along with the suspension, the probation?"

"I think so. You need to forget this Ayn Rand approach. Look, Howard Roark could have built a heck of a lot more buildings if he'd compromised a little. And you're not John Galt; you can't just drop out. You're a physician, for heaven's sake."

"How did you know I liked Ayn Rand?"

"Wasn't hard. Pretty obvious, really."

"So what would you do?"

"Hmmm. I don't know what I would do. I haven't really thought about it." Jack pushed his chair back from the microscope and looked at the ceiling, looked around a little, shrugged, and said nothing for about a minute. Then he said, "The most important thing is that your name doesn't end up in the National Practitioner Data Bank. If you appeal, and lose, which you will, and are suspended from the medical staff and put on probation, all that is reported to the Data Bank. Then for the rest of your life you'll have to explain that – every time you renew your medical license, every time you apply for medical staff privileges, here or anywhere…you have to explain what happened. And even when you explain everything, it will *still* be held against you."

"Yeah."

"Soooo, what I would do, I think, and what I recommend is…that you cut a deal, something like this: You tell the Executive Committee that you will voluntarily leave for three weeks – call it a vacation. And accept the probation for the three years, again voluntarily, so it doesn't go to the board, so it's not official, and it's not reportable to the Data Bank. Give up all your appeals, all your rights to counsel and all that stuff, so that everything is voluntary. Then sign whatever the Executive Committee wants you to sign, and do whatever they tell you to do – get counseling from Dr. Todd, go to 'anger management meetings'…whatever."

"I don't need help."

"Who cares! The thing is, if you do things this way, none of it is reportable to anyone. It's all voluntary. I'm talking about preserving your career."

"Again, why are you doing this?"

"I already told you. I want to look at the specimens you send me."

"Seriously. Why?"

"Okay. I'll tell you why. There was this one time I was talking to Steve Prescott, and we were talking about gastrointestinal disease and gastroenterologists. I was curious, and I asked Steve who he used as a consultant when he needed to send patients to a gastroenterologist – you or your ex-partners. He said that if the problem was something routine and easy to handle, he sent the patient to your ex-partners; if it was something that required some thought and judgment, he sent the patient to you. And he's not the only one who thinks that way. Every physician here thinks that way. *That's* why I want you around."

"I'll think about your suggestions."

Dr. Benson thought about Jack's suggestions for about five minutes. Jack was talking sense. Dr. Benson was no quitter, but he was not going to win this fight, and if he continued along this course, well, he could lose everything. He called his attorney, Jason Price, and convinced him to sign off on what Jack suggested. It wasn't hard.

Jason Price said, "Sure, I'll write it up. Actually, I've been thinking it over and doing some research. The laws have changed, and the hospitals have a real advantage in these matters. Judges and juries tend to go with patient safety first, and doctors' rights second. Actually, it's like you have no rights. I'm not sure you would win an appeal. In fact, you'd probably lose."

Then Dr. Benson phoned Dr. Rickert and outlined his proposal.

Dr. Rickert said that he liked it, to make everything voluntary – no appeals, no more called meetings with lawyers and administrators, no more ticked-off doctors – what was not to like?

"Put it in writing," said Dr. Rickert.

"I will," said Dr. Benson.

"No guarantees, but I think I can get the administration, the Executive Committee, and the board to go along with it. *But* you have to follow through this time. This is your last chance."

"Okay."

It had been a long day, one of the longest of Morris Benson's life. It wasn't over. He drove home in his 1989 Mercedes Coupe, to his house on Cherokee Drive in the Openwood subdivision. It was a short drive. Every drive in Siegeburg was a short drive.

Gladys Nelson, a pediatric nurse, was still there. Nurse Nelson was African American, with grown kids. She took care of Tommy, Dr. Benson's nine-year-old boy, his only child, who was autistic and required

round-the-clock care. Tommy's mother had died of breast cancer the previous year – she used to take care of Tommy. Now Gladys did. As a
specialist, a pediatric nurse, Gladys's care was expensive. She was worth it.

"How was Tommy today?" asked Dr. Benson.

"Okay," said Nurse Nelson, "about the same as always. We had
some vegetable soup for lunch. He spent the day watching TV. No outbursts or anything, a pretty uneventful day, really."

"Thanks. I'll take it from here. Did you want to stay for dinner?"

"No. I have to get home. I'll see you tomorrow morning."

"Okay. We can talk then. I have some stuff to take care of tomorrow. Then Tommy and I may go on a vacation for a few weeks."

"No problem."

After seeing Ms. Nelson out and thanking her, Dr. Benson walked
upstairs and looked into Tommy's room. He was sitting on his bed,
watching TV, where the cartoon channel was blazing away. Tommy was
a cute kid, like all nine-year-old boys, with blond hair, just like his mom.
In fact, he looked very much like his mom.

Everything stable, Dr. Benson walked downstairs to the kitchen and
turned the oven to 350 degrees. When the oven reached that temp, he
smeared a couple of potatoes with butter, wrapped them in aluminum foil,
and put them in the oven to bake. With that part of the meal started, he
went into the den/TV room and read the *Siegeburg Post* and the *Wall
Street Journal.* When Morris finished his reading, he walked to the backyard patio, turned on the natural gas to the grill, and fired it up. He
checked on the potatoes, which were doing fine. He took two T-bone
steaks out of the refrigerator, salted them, and put them on the grill. He
cooked the steaks for a total of seven minutes; Morris and his son liked
their steaks quite rare. Dr. Benson took the steaks off the grill, put them
on a serving plate, closed the grill and turned off the gas. He brought the
steaks into the kitchen, took the potatoes out of the oven, and matched
the meat and potatoes, one set on each plate. Morris put a plate on each
of the two TV trays in the den. He went upstairs to get Tommy. He sat
Tommy down in front of his TV tray and poured him some milk. Dr.
Benson had a beer. Dr. Benson cut up some of the meat and potatoes into
small bites for Tommy. At first Tommy rocked and flapped instead of
eating. Dr. Benson turned the TV to the cartoon channel. Tommy calmed

down and seemed satisfied and took a few bites of food with his spoon. Dr. Benson enjoyed his meat and potatoes, cooked to perfection. He took his knife and fork and cut some more bites of the steak and potato for his son. Things were peaceful and quiet other than the faint noise from the TV, which had the volume turned low. Tommy was content – eating and attentive to the TV. Dr. Benson opened his briefcase and took out the latest issue of the *New England Journal of Medicine*. As he ate, he read a wonderful review of the new nomenclature for colonic polyps.

Both escaped into their perfect worlds.

A PREDICTION

Friday, January 22, 1991

3:00 P.M.

Ellen Murtaugh calmly said, "Please do something. Otherwise I will die in the next hour."

This was said in the Intensive Care Unit of the Medical University of South Carolina, a teaching hospital in Charleston. Ellen Murtaugh, the patient, was a seventy-seven-year-old woman with an appearance consistent with her age. She was slim with long gray hair and a gentle countenance. Her daughter, Dr. Diane Murtaugh, a pediatrician in her early forties, sat at her bedside.

Ellen Murtaugh had been admitted the previous day because of the sudden onset of a little weakness in her right hand – she couldn't close her fingers together. The diagnosis was a mild stroke. She was treated with baby aspirin and admitted to the Medical Intensive Care Unit (MICU), not because she needed "intensive care," but as a precaution. There was no reason for anyone to think that she would die anytime soon, certainly not within an hour. There was nothing life threatening about her condition at all.

The day before, when Dr. Diane Murtaugh had received the phone call telling her that her mother was in the hospital, she immediately threw a few things into a suitcase and drove from Siegeburg, Tennessee, to Charleston and went straight to the hospital. Dr. Murtaugh and Ellen Murtaugh had a daughter-mother relationship, not a doctor-patient relationship, but Dr. Murtaugh was having trouble discerning that. Her mother needed an internist or a hospitalist or a neurologist – not a pediatrician. Dr. Murtaugh didn't even have a medical license to practice in South Carolina, only Tennessee. A medical license is not like a driver's license, which can be used to drive a car in another state; to practice medicine in South Carolina, Dr. Murtaugh needed a South Carolina medical license.

Once on-site Dr. Murtaugh was either at her mother's bedside or in the waiting room just outside the MICU. She dozed off a little from time to time, but didn't really sleep, and she was exhausted. But Dr. Murtaugh had no plans to leave or take a break. She was a doctor and invulnerable. She would sleep later, when her mother was well again.

But her mother would never be well again. She said again, "Please do something, or I will die in the next hour."

Dr. Murtaugh panicked. Then she took charge. She shouted orders at the centrally located nursing station, but no one was there – the clerk was taking a break. The MICU nurses were in patients' rooms, taking care of, well, patients. Each room had clear floor-to-ceiling windows so the nurses could keep an eye on their patients even if they weren't in the room. Therefore, all the nurses, patients, and visitors observed Dr. Murtaugh as she marched to and around the nursing station, gesticulating and shouting orders, like General Patton rallying the troops.

"I want a CT of the head and an MRI stat!" commanded Dr. Murtaugh. "And I want a heparin drip with a baseline PTT!"

Shirley Joiner, the nursing supervisor, intercepted Dr. Murtaugh, gently took her by the elbow, and guided her back to her mother's room. The two women were about the same age. Nurse Joiner was a strong blond woman, almost six feet tall.

"What are you doing?" shouted Dr. Murtaugh. "Get radiology up here, stat!"

"Keep your voice down," whispered Ms. Joiner. "There are other patients here, you know. What's the problem?"

Dr. Murtaugh blurted out, "My mother is dying!"

Nurse Joiner checked Ellen Murtaugh's pulse oximeter – 97.5, normal. The EKG monitor showed a normal pattern. To document this Shirley pressed PRINT, and a strip of paper recorded the normal tracing. The monitors showed a blood pressure of 111/72 and a pulse of 70, both normal. Nurse Joiner felt Ellen Murtaugh's wrist, and the pulse was strong and regular. She checked the IV line, which was hooked up to a pump buzzing in the background. The volume of the buzzing varied, so the effect was like that of a mosquito that flies close and then flies away. The pump was set to deliver normal saline at the rate of 60 ccs an hour through an IV line inserted in the skin at the back of the patient's left wrist. Ms. Joiner checked the IV – no leakage, no infiltration, no bleeding, and no problem. What was going on?

So Shirley asked exactly that: "What's going on?"

Dr. Murtaugh said, "My mother…"

"Not you," said Ms. Joiner to Dr. Murtaugh. "I'm talking to the patient."

"What's going on?" Nurse Joiner repeated.

Ellen Murtaugh said, "I'm going to die in the next hour."

The nurse shook her head in disbelief. "I don't understand. Everything's normal. Does anything hurt?"

"No."

"Then how do you know you will die in the next hour?"

"I just know."

"Do you have a headache?"

"No."

"Chest pain?"

"No."

"Pain anywhere?"

"No."

"Then why do you say you're going to die soon?"

"Within the hour."

"Right. Why do you say that?"

"I just know."

Dr. Murtaugh watched her mother breathe, in no distress whatsoever. In fact, as her mother made her pronouncements of impending death, she was quite calm and matter of fact about it, even while asking for help. Ellen Murtaugh said to her daughter, "Everything is so intense, so vivid, when you face death. You are such a beautiful woman, you know that, don't you? I'm so proud of you."

"That's not important," said Dr. Murtaugh. "We need to find your doctor."

Ellen Murtaugh said, "That's Adrian Finch, you remember him, your old high school sweetheart?"

"That's not important," said Dr. Murtaugh. "He just needs to get here."

3:10 P.M.

"Where's radiology!?" asked Dr. Murtaugh.

"We haven't called them yet," said Ms. Joiner.

"What! I ordered a CT and MRI fifteen minutes ago. Where's the lab? I need that PTT drawn NOW so I can start the heparin drip."

"None of that is going to happen until her doctor orders it, and you're not her doctor."

"Well, at least call Dr. Finch. Get him over here!"

"Okay." Shirley Joiner went to the nursing station to make the call.

Dr. Adrian Finch did not have far to come. He was an internist. He was making rounds, so he was already in the hospital. Adrian Finch was a jovial guy of average height, with a ready smile, which showed well-maintained teeth. He dressed with Southern gentility – a white lab coat, white shirt and black tie with white dots. His brown hair was parted on the left, combed to the right. He wore wire-frame glasses with golden rims. He came from a medical family. His father was an internist and a writer, a good writer actually, who was in the South Carolina Writers Hall of Fame, whose books were about a physician remarkably similar to the author. Dr. Adrian Finch was not a writer, just a doctor, an internist, and proud of it.

Dr. Finch hurried to Ellen Murtaugh's bedside. Not only was she Dr. Finch's patient, but Ellen Murtaugh was a family friend. For that matter, so was Dr. Diane Murtaugh. In fact, he had loved her in high school – and still did. The feeling was not mutual.

As far as Dr. Finch could tell, Diane Murtaugh had changed amazingly little since high school. She weighed the same, still had a great figure, and outstanding legs, which she always showed off with knee-length dresses. She never wore slacks.

"Are you still a pediatrician?" he asked.

"Yeah."

"You married yet?"

"No."

"Got any kids?"

"No. I don't have time. I work over eighty hours a week. I'm the only pediatrician in Siegeburg. Enough about that. Check on my mother."

Dr. Finch reluctantly turned his attention to Ellen Murtaugh. He observed a patient in no apparent distress. Then he asked her, "How are you?"

"She says she's going to die," said Dr. Murtaugh.

Dr. Finch ignored Dr. Murtaugh and again addressed his patient: "What's going on?"

"I'm going to die within the hour."

"How do you know that?"

"I just know."

"Do you hurt anywhere?"

"No."

"Do you have a headache? Any chest pain?"

"No."

Dr. Finch took out his stethoscope and listened to Ellen Murtaugh's heart and lungs, the ticktock of the heart, and the wind going in and out of the lungs – nothing amiss. When he was finished, he leaned back and stood up straight, satisfied. "Sounds good," he said. "I think you'll be fine." He started to leave the room.

"Stop!" said Dr. Murtaugh. "You're not going to do anything?"

"Nothing *to* do. Your mom's stable. I looked at her labs this morning. She's a little anemic, hemoglobin around 11. Otherwise her labs are fantastic. She'll probably outlive us all."

"She's had a stroke. She needs a CT and an MRI."

"We did all that yesterday, and they didn't show much."

"She needs a PTT, and then start a heparin drip."

"That's not a good idea. In fact, it's a bad idea."

"Do it!"

"Look," said Dr. Finch. "There are risks to starting heparin, like bleeding, like hemorrhage in the brain, which is the last thing your mom needs. You're a doctor. You *know* that. Or should know that."

"I want a neurologist to see her, now."

"Fine. I'll get a neurology consult, but I don't think that's going to change anything. Look, I need to get going." Once again, he tried to leave.

"No," said Dr. Murtaugh. "You're staying right here." She grabbed Dr. Finch's arm.

"Let go of my arm."

"No!"

Dr. Finch jerked his arm free. "If you assault me again, I'm calling security."

"You're taking this out on me and my family because I rejected you."

"That's ridiculous. That was high school stuff. I have to get to work." He walked out of the room and out of the MICU.

3:20 P.M.

Dr. Murtaugh sat with her mother for a minute and then walked to the nursing station. She directed her comments to the clerk, Angela Morehead, who was a short, perky, slim, cute redhead sitting at the desk with a pile of medical charts in front of her.

Dr. Murtaugh said, "I still want radiology up here, stat. And a phlebotomist from the lab."

"I'll have to get the nursing supervisor," said Angela.

Angela walked away with quick short steps to another patient's room and came back with Shirley Joiner, who said, "What now?"

Dr. Murtaugh said, "I'm asking, and I will keep asking, for something to be done about my mother. She needs…"

"You don't have medical privileges here," said Ms. Joiner.

"So what. I'm a doctor. I'm the patient's daughter."

Shirley Joiner shook her head. "I've had enough of this," she said. "I'm calling administration."

"What! Waste some more time?"

Shirley Joiner walked from the nursing station to the nurses break room, a small sparsely furnished room with a refrigerator, table and chairs, coffee maker, and a phone. Shirley picked up the phone and punched in four numbers. The administrative assistant of the executive suite, Alice Haines, answered the call.

"I need some help," said Shirley.

"What's the problem?" asked Alice.

"I have a disruptive physician who's not even on staff here. Is Mr. Jones there?" Reginald Jones was the CEO.

"He's gone for the day," said Alice. Of course he was. It was Friday afternoon.

"How about Janice Bradshaw?" asked Shirley. Janice Bradshaw was the chief operating officer.

"I'll connect you."

Shirley Joiner told Janice Bradshaw what was going on.

"Do you want me to come over there?" asked Janice.

"Yes, otherwise I'm calling security."

"I'll be right over."

Shirley Joiner walked back to the nursing station and told Dr. Murtaugh that someone from administration was coming over.

"Good," said Dr. Murtaugh.

"I don't think you are going to like it," said Shirley.

The COO, Janice Bradshaw, was a no-nonsense dark-haired woman of about forty years of age. She played lacrosse when she was in college. She entered the MICU and went to the nursing station, where she exchanged a few words with Shirley Joiner – very few words, before they were interrupted by Dr. Murtaugh, who left her mother's side to butt in.

"When are you going to do something to help my mother?" Dr. Murtaugh asked the two women.

Janice Bradshaw introduced herself. "We are helping your mother – the nurses, Ms. Joiner, Dr. Finch – everyone is trying to help your mother."

"But they're not doing what I ask," said Dr. Murtaugh.

"What are they not doing?" asked Janice.

"I've been asking for radiology, for lab…for about an hour. Nothing is happening."

"I'll talk to Dr. Finch about that," said Janice.

"Save your breath. I don't care what he says. What I am asking for needs to be done. I'm a doctor."

"You're not on the medical staff here."

"I know what I'm doing."

Dr. Murtaugh went behind the nursing desk and grabbed her mother's chart from the chart rack. "I'm documenting this," she said. "I'm going to write the orders myself."

"You're out of line," said Shirley Joiner. She moved close to Dr. Murtaugh to get the chart back. Dr. Murtaugh pushed her away.

Janice Bradshaw picked up the phone and paged Dr. Finch.

3:30 P.M.

Once again it did not take long for Dr. Finch to get to the MICU. He saw Dr. Murtaugh at the chart rack, reading her mother's medical record. Janice Bradshaw and Shirley Joiner had backed off. Two MICU nurses stood behind them, wondering what was going to happen next. They'd never seen anything like it.

Dr. Finch walked to where Dr. Murtaugh was standing, grabbed the chart, and put it back in the rack. "That's enough," said Dr. Finch.

"You mean I can't see my mother's chart?"

"Fine! Here you go."

He gave it back. Dr. Murtaugh resumed looking at it. "She's anemic," said Dr. Murtaugh.

"I told you that earlier," said Dr. Finch.

"Well, do something," said Dr. Murtaugh.

Shaking his head, Dr. Finch led everyone over to Ellen Murtaugh's bedside. "How are you feeling?" he asked his patient.

"Have you found out why I'm going to die?"

Dr. Finch answered with a shake of his head. He looked at the monitors. Vital signs were normal. He turned to Shirley Joiner and said, "Everything seems fine. Still, let's get a crash cart handy, just as a precaution."

Shirley and another nurse went to get the crash cart. Dr. Murtaugh tagged along and helped. They rolled the specialized metallic cuboidal red cart to Ellen Murtaugh's bedside, which wasn't easy – it was about chest high and kind of heavy. The cart was subdivided into six drawers. The top drawer was filled with an intubation kit. The remaining drawers were filled with drugs used for resuscitation.

Shirley told Dr. Murtaugh, "Thanks for the help. You have to go now. Visiting hours are over."

"Thank God," said Dr. Finch.

"I'm not going anywhere," said Dr. Murtaugh.

"Look," said Shirley. "Visiting hours in the ICU are 1:30 to 3:30. You know that. You can come back in at 5:30."

"I'm not leaving."

"Look, please try to cooperate. At four o'clock there's a shift change, and the nurses here now have to go over their patients with the nurses on the next shift, to coordinate care. You're a doctor. You know that."

Dr. Finch gently took Dr. Murtaugh's left arm to escort her out. Dr. Murtaugh slapped him across the face with her right hand. "I'm not leaving," she said.

Dr. Finch backed off, shook his head, and walked away. He joined Janice Bradshaw at the nursing station, and the two walked out of the MICU.

That left Shirley Joiner and Dr. Murtaugh at an impasse. They stared each other down, neither one moving.

3:40 P.M.

Dr. Finch re-entered the MICU and walked to Ellen Murtaugh's room. The patient was resting quietly. Dr. Murtaugh was anxiously watching her. Shirley Joiner had returned to the nursing station to get ready for the shift change at the top of the hour.

To say "death is a mystery" is to render a tautology. No one *knows* what happens to a person when that person dies.

But even physiological death itself, the actual dying, the pathophysiology of death, which one would think would be rational, biochemical, anatomic, scientific – well, often that's a mystery as well. Death often eludes a medical/scientific explanation. Oh, we say a person dies of "cancer," but that's not really the case. The tumor load on the day of death is not perceptibly more than the preceding day, when the patient was alive. We say a patient dies of a heart attack, and that's kind of true. Still it is not predictable whether or not a heart attack that occurs secondary to a certain thrombus in a certain coronary artery will kill a specific patient or not – some live, and some die, and it's usually a mystery which heart attack patients live and which die. The course of an infection is unpredictable; some patients die of pneumonia, some don't, and predicting who will live and who will not is impossible.

Any pathologist with autopsy experience will tell you almost all of the time we know what a patient dies *with*, not what a patient dies *from*.

Death can come suddenly and violently, or death can come quietly like a whisper that drifts off to silence. It can come with fanfare or totally out of the blue. Either way, predicting the exact time and manner of death is impossible. Never happens.

On the other hand.

Experienced doctors will tell you that a patient usually knows his or her diagnosis before the doctor does. If a patient says he has lung cancer, I assure you that the most expensive radiologic and pathologic studies in the world will merely confirm it. If a patient tells the doctor that she has the flu, in most cases Tamiflu will fix that patient right up.

And there are rare times, as with Ellen Murtaugh, when a patient with no objective evidence whatsoever predicts his or her own demise, often within minutes of when it actually happens. Older doctors will tell you that it *does* happen.

As Ellen Murtaugh predicted, she just up and died.

But not without a fight from Dr. Diane Murtaugh. "Call a code!" she screamed.

Nurse Joiner shouted to the MICU clerk to do so. Almost immediately the message CODE BLUE MICU, CODE BLUE MICU, CODE BLUE MICU blared over all the loudspeakers in the hospital.

Dr. Murtaugh opened her mother's mouth and with her right hand tried to clear out any secretions and then used her left hand to arch her mother's neck – all this to make sure Ellen Murtaugh had an open airway. Then Dr. Murtaugh used her left hand to pinch her mother's nostrils shut. Diane Murtaugh gave her mother five quick breaths, mouth to mouth. Ellen Murtaugh's chest rose and fell with each breath. Then Dr. Murtaugh moved to her mom's chest and applied compressions to the sternum, as fast and as hard as she was able. Everyone except Dr. Murtaugh could hear the resultant breaking ribs.

When there is a code, everything seems to happen at once, and chaos rules. What happens during a code during a TV hospital drama is pretty much the way it happens in real life. A screenwriter really doesn't have to punch it up much – after all, the stakes are pretty high as it is, life and death.

However, what may or may not be evident on resuscitation as acted out on a TV show is this: one person has to be in charge. Otherwise everyone is running around yelling stat this and stat that, with no coordination or cohesiveness. If no one is in charge, or even worse, if several doctors try to run things, the results are catastrophic.

Dr. Finch rushed to the bedside and pulled Dr. Murtaugh away from her mother and shoved her aside. "Let me do my job," he said. He took over the chest compressions.

Dr. Murtaugh used the momentum to get to the crash cart. She grabbed a laryngoscope and endotracheal tube before anyone could stop her.

"She's my mother," she said. Dr. Murtaugh shoved the laryngoscope into her mother's mouth and throat and guided the endotracheal tube down toward the chest, aiming for the larynx and trachea.

She missed. The endotracheal tube went down the esophagus instead, a suboptimal result to say the least. So when Dr. Murtaugh hooked up the endotracheal tube to the ambu bag and compressed the ambu bag to get air to the lungs, the air went to the stomach instead. That was no help.

Dr. Finch stopped the chest compressions, took the stethoscope out of his lab coat, and listened to the patient's chest as Dr. Murtaugh repeatedly squeezed the ambu bag and then released it, trying ineffectively to get some air to her mother's lungs. Didn't happen. As Dr. Finch listened through his stethoscope, he heard a horrible nothing, no air coming in and out. Right chest, silence. Left chest, silence. Elvis had left the building.

Dr. Finch said, "I'll have to start over." He pulled the endotracheal tube out of the patient's stomach, esophagus, and mouth. He inserted the laryngoscope and prepared to put the endo**tracheal** tube in its proper place, the **trachea**.

Dr. Murtaugh went back to compressing her mother's chest, trying to take the place of the non-beating heart, breaking more ribs in the process.

Nurse Joiner said, "You're pressing too hard. Let me do it."

"No," said Dr. Murtaugh. "I'll worry about the broken ribs later. Right now we need to pump blood."

Two people from the respiratory care team showed up, both young men. Dr. Finch finally got the endotracheal tube where it was supposed to be. He taped it in place and attached it to a respirator. With a functioning airway, one respiratory therapist started fiddling with the supplemental oxygen settings.

The lungs were taken care of. Ellen Murtaugh was getting air and oxygen. Now attention was focused on the heart. Dr. Murtaugh was *still* doing chest compressions – not in a very nice way, and not in a very effective way.

Dr. Finch said to Dr. Murtaugh, "Let me take over."

"No," said Dr. Murtaugh.

"Good grief," said Dr. Finch. "You're impairing her chances."

"Get me some blood gases!" yelled Dr. Murtaugh.

Not knowing any better, a respiratory therapist, the one not minding the ventilator, drew some blood from the femoral artery in the right groin. He put the syringe with blood on ice and left to run the tests.

A phlebotomist from the lab showed up with her cart of needles, syringes and tubes. Dr. Murtaugh told her, "I want a sodium, potassium, CO2, glucose, lactate, and pH."

Word of the Code Blue had gotten around. Ellen Murtaugh's room was like Grand Central Station. A cardiologist showed up, a gray-haired man. "Who's in charge?" he asked.

"I am," said Dr. Murtaugh.

"Who are you?"

"She's the patient's daughter," said Dr. Finch. "I'm in charge, or at least trying to be."

"Okay," said the cardiologist. He looked at the EKG on the monitor. There wasn't much to see. It was a flat line.

Dr. Finch said, "Ampule of epinephrine, please."

The cardiologist nodded agreement.

Nurse Joiner took a little flask-shaped glass bottle of epinephrine out of the crash cart, broke off the top, used a needle to draw out the contents into a syringe, removed the needle, and flushed the drug into the intravenous line.

Dr. Murtaugh continued to pound her mother's chest, continued breaking ribs.

Shirley Joiner took the defibrillator and paddles out of the crash cart, hoping that Ellen Murtaugh would go into some sort of heart rhythm that they could shock into normal sinus rhythm, the key word of that phrase being "normal," as in normal heart function. But to do that they needed ventricular flutter, ventricular tachycardia, ventricular fibrillation…something, anything, but what was there was nothing – asystole, a flat line on the EKG monitor, the most depressing image in medicine.

They did four more cycles of epinephrine. Three of the cycles were epinephrine delivered into the intravenous line. The last cycle consisted of the cardiologist injecting the epinephrine directly into the left heart itself, via a long needle into the chest. During that last attempt, Dr. Murtaugh finally stopped the chest compressions.

Nothing worked. The EKG remained a flat line, asystole, no heartbeat, no activity, nothing…it was over.

4:05 P.M.

Dr. Finch said, "I'm calling it."

"NO!" screamed Dr. Murtaugh.

"It's been twenty-five minutes. We're not getting any response. Nothing."

"I'm not giving up. Let's try amiodarone, once, one ampule."

Dr. Finch nodded to Shirley Joiner. "Give the patient an ampule of amiodarone."

Nurse Joiner did so – same procedure as for the IV epinephrine – out of the bottle, into the syringe, into the IV line, into the patient.

Same result. Nothing happened.

Dr. Finch said, "It's over. I'm calling it. We've done all we can."

"Let's try something else," said Dr. Murtaugh.

The respiratory therapist shut off the oxygen and started to disconnect the endotracheal tube from the respirator. "Don't you unhook that oxygen!" Dr. Murtaugh said to the respiratory therapist. "She needs it." Dr. Murtaugh pushed him away and hooked up the respirator to the endotracheal tube.

Dr. Murtaugh sobbed. Shirley Joiner removed the IV needle from the patient's left antecubital region. Dr. Murtaugh grabbed the needle and tried to reinsert it where it was, and stuck herself in the palm of her left hand with the needle. Blood dripped from Dr. Murtaugh's hand and mixed with the blood on Ellen Murtaugh's skin, where the IV had been. "She needs this IV," said Dr. Murtaugh as she tried to restart it, jabbing frantically into her mother's skin where the IV had been inserted. After a few tries she dropped the needle and cried in frustration.

Four really big men arrived at the MICU and entered Ellen Murtaugh's room. They were accompanied by Janice Bradshaw. The four men were Reginald Jones (the CEO of the hospital), the chief of the medical staff, the head of hospital security, and a member of the Charleston Police Department, who was actually off-duty, but moonlighted as a security officer for the Medical University of South Carolina. The police officer and head of security pulled Dr. Murtaugh's arms behind her and handcuffed her wrists.

"What are you doing?" shouted Dr. Murtaugh as she struggled to free herself. It wasn't much of a struggle. The head of security and the police officer were not only big, they were strong and experienced. They had handled much bigger and tougher offenders.

"I'm committing you to psychiatric," said Dr. Finch.

"What!? You can't do that."

"Actually, I can, and I did. For your own good. You are out of control. You need some medicine, some counseling, some care. In your condition I'm afraid you will hurt yourself or others. You need help."

The head of hospital security took Dr. Murtaugh's left arm, and the police officer took the right arm, and they marched Dr. Murtaugh to the locked psychiatric ward of the Medical University of South Carolina. Dr. Murtaugh shook her head in disbelief the whole way. At the end of the short journey was a locked patient room. Dr. Murtaugh sat on the bed, more alone than she had ever been in her whole life.

4:10 P.M.

Ellen Murtaugh was pronounced dead by Dr. Finch. He walked to the nursing station, sat down, and did the paperwork:

Manner of Death: Natural.

Cause of Death: Unknown.

THE WOMAN WHO TALKED TOO FAST

Sunday, June 13, 1991

I was reclining next to my backyard pool on a Sunday afternoon when the phone rang. I answered it because I was on call.

A woman said, "Hello, Jack?"

"Yeah."

"It's Diane Murtaugh."

Diane was a pediatrician at Excel McClain Hospital. My initial worry was that she had a patient she wanted help with – maybe look at a peripheral blood smear of one of her patients. Then I remembered that I hadn't seen her for a while.

"What's going on?" I said.

Diane talked fast, too fast: "My problems began when my mother had a stroke in Charleston. She could talk, but she had some weakness in her right hand. But she was just lying there, like a little girl. Do you know how hard it was for me to see her like that? Can you imagine what that was like? This was a woman, a woman who had always been in perfect health. My father is frail, has been for several years – I would expect something like this from him. But my mother? I dropped everything and drove to Charleston, the first time I've deserted my patients, who are my children. I've become the complete physician, taking care not only of their bodies, but their minds and souls. Have you read *The Cunning Man* by Robertson Davies?"

"I..."

"Well," she interrupted, "that's what I am, a 'cunning woman' – I take complete care of my patients. Most patients are as sick in their heads as they are in their bodies, you know what I'm saying?"

"I…"

"I don't really practice 'alternative medicine' though. After all, I am an AOA graduate of Ivory Medical School. But I'm also on the Siegeburg School Board. I make sure that my patients do well in school, and when they do, I give them presents – teddy bears, model airplanes, running shoes, basketballs, dolls – when they get good grades. My attic is a toy store. My downstairs is a combination medical office/living room. I'm always on call."

I said, "You may be overextended."

"No. I'm fine."

"Why are you calling me?"

"My problems began when my mother had a stroke in Charleston…"

I interrupted: "You said that." She was still talking too fast.

"I drove straight to the hospital. I went to her room, in the MICU. I talked to the nurses. I went to the nursing station…"

"Where you were very nice, I hope."

"I was. I just wanted to know why her labs weren't back. I also wanted a CT scan of her head and an MRI and a heparin drip with a baseline PTT."

"Oh."

"They wouldn't do it."

"Diane, you're a pediatrician, not a neurologist. Are you even licensed in South Carolina?"

"No, that's what *they* said. But the patient was my mother. Before I could go to administration and get temporary privileges or something, she died, right there in the unit, while I was there."

She finally stopped talking. I said, "I can't imagine how horrible that must have been."

"You have no idea. Then I couldn't even make arrangements for the funeral or take care of my mom's affairs, because I was committed to a locked psychiatric unit. My younger brother had to take care of everything."

"That's bizarre."

"You probably heard about it. Did you know that in the state of South Carolina, one physician can commit you to a mental institution for up to five days?"

"I think that's the case in many states, including Tennessee."

"The one who did that, he's an old enemy, who chose now to strike. He's been mad at me ever since high school when I rebuffed his advances. HIGH SCHOOL!"

"Diane," I said gently, "you are not making sense. Who is this 'old enemy'?"

"His name is Adrian Finch," she said rapidly. "I knew him in high school, and for a while we dated seriously, but then we broke up, and I went to college, and then I wanted to get back together again, but he didn't want to, and then later he wanted to get back together with me, and I didn't want to, and he never got over that. He chose now to get even."

"Amazing how these things can come back to haunt you," I said.

"It was illegal, what he did to me, to commit me, you know what I'm saying? In South Carolina, one doctor, who doesn't even have to be a psychiatrist, can commit you to a mental hospital *for five days*. It took me three days and seven thousand dollars in legal fees to get out."

"Wow."

"My nightmare wasn't over. When I got home, I couldn't work at my hospital. Bryan Magnuson, Kathy Lassiter, and Aaron Rickert wouldn't let me in the hospital. The Siegeburg sheriff, Lanny...I can't remember his last name, was at the entrance to the hospital. The sheriff said there was a restraining order; they said I was a risk to patients...ME! A RISK!?"

"Your own hospital turned on you."

"They did."

Actually, I wasn't too surprised. Dr. Diane Murtaugh had alienated a lot of people. Rob Masterson, an ob-gyn doc, was angry at her because Dr. Murtaugh told a mother that her newborn would have a lower IQ because of the anesthetic agents Dr. Rob Masterson used during labor and delivery. When Rob told me about it, he said, "That was a good way to make an enemy of a colleague."

Then there was the time a friend of Diane's was treated for ovarian cancer by Dr. Rickert. The cancer was cured, but one of the chemotherapeutic agents Dr. Rickert used caused a neuropathy. Dr. Murtaugh convinced her friend to sue Dr. Rickert for malpractice. Dr. Rickert won the case, but it took several years of hassle. Dr. Rickert told me he would never be the same again, told me: "I saved her friend's life and got sued for it." And that's how Diane alienated Dr. Aaron Rickert, the chief of the medical staff, who was quite happy to enforce the restraining order keeping Dr. Murtaugh out of the hospital. There would be no help from him.

Until Diane's phone call, I hadn't heard a thing about any of this, perhaps because the actions against Dr. Murtaugh were legal matters, not medical matters, and confidential.

I was perplexed – was Dr. Murtaugh turning to me for help? So I asked her: "What is it that you want me to do?"

"Everything will be in the packet," said Diane.

"What packet?"

"The one that I am mailing to you."

"But what is it you want me to *do*?"

"It'll all be in the packet."

Two days later the packet showed up in the mail, but what Diane wanted me to do was *not* in the packet. It did contain a lot of interesting stuff though. It was huge, two inches thick, but well organized; there was even a table of contents:

1. Newspaper clippings
2. Curriculum vitae
3. Pertinent Material from the National Practitioner Data Bank
4. Records from the Department of Health
5. Disputed Adverse Decisions
6. Disputed Diagnosis
7. Copy of Page 26 of the Tennessee Codes Annotated Covering Evaluation Process for a Licensed Physicians
8. Conflicts of Interest of an Attorney from the General Counsel's Office of the Health Licensing Board
9. Civil Liberties
10. Summary

It took me an entire afternoon to read it. Briefly, this is what happened:

The bizarre story began with a trip by Dr. Diane Murtaugh to Charleston, South Carolina, to see her mother in the hospital. While she was there, Dr. Adrian Finch, an internist, committed her to a psychiatric ward with a diagnosis of bipolar disorder, a diagnosis that Diane vehemently disagreed with. She was taken to the ward by force, locked up, and held there against her will. She and her attorney were able to obtain her release after three days. Then Dr. Murtaugh returned to Siegeburg, only to find that her privileges at Excel McClain Hospital were suspended because of the Charleston incident. Dr. Murtaugh resumed practicing pediatrics out of her office, but she couldn't admit patients to the hospital. However, even her office practice was stopped after a few weeks when the Tennessee Department of Health Licensing Board charged her with "practicing medicine when physically and mentally unable to safely do so," and suspended her Tennessee medical license. The licensing board regarded the diagnosis of bipolar disorder as applicable to her mental fitness to practice medicine. She was directed to meet with Dr. Patrick Todd, the director of the state Impaired Physicians Health Program, for evaluation, counseling, and treatment; in the meantime Dr. Murtaugh was prohibited from the practice of medicine.

This adverse information was reported to the National Practitioner Data Bank, which keeps track of the misdeeds of physicians. Whenever a physician applies for medical privileges anywhere – a hospital, physicians' group, state licensing board, insurance company – that entity queries the National Practitioner Data Bank, and there it is – a record of what adverse information has been reported about that physician. It's like a Scarlet Letter that follows a physician around for the rest of his or her career.

Diane Murtaugh, M.D., didn't go along with any of this, but fought the authorities every step of the way.

In particular, Dr. Murtaugh's meeting with Dr. Patrick Todd, the physician in charge of the state's Impaired Physician Program, went very badly. As far as Dr. Murtaugh was concerned, the agenda of the meeting was to correct the erroneous record that she was bipolar; Dr. Todd's agenda was to help Dr. Murtaugh get treatment for an established diagnosis of bipolar disorder. Not surprisingly, with two such different agendas, the meeting resulted in no agreement about anything. For his part, Dr. Todd confirmed the bipolar disorder diagnosis and recommended to Dr. Murtaugh, and the licensing board, that she undergo treatment by a psychiatrist approved by Dr. Todd and the licensing board.

Dr. Murtaugh totally rejected this course of action: In chapter six of the packet with a title "Disputed Diagnosis" there was a copy of a letter from Dr. Murtaugh to Dr. Todd and the licensing board, which said: "I have no intention of being retooled and refitted into a generic human being and physician brainwashed with beliefs and standards that are the latest fads of the psychiatric and medical community. I think their obsessive search for normality is actually a quest for conformity, which is detrimental to society, my patients, and me. Only death or dismemberment would be worse."

I thought what Diane said had merit, but would not help her get what she wanted – to resume her pediatric practice. Diane's iconoclastic ideas might be valid, or even helpful for creative endeavors like music, art, or writing – but for a guild like medicine – or law, teaching, accounting, the clergy or any profession for that matter – it's conform or you're out.

The hard lesson to learn, then, is that to survive as a professional, you have to give up some of your individuality, your autonomy, and even some of your humanity, to survive. I'm not sure those who enter professional schools realize this. Warning signs should be posted at the entrances.

No one ever told all this to Diane Murtaugh. Even when I knew her in medical school, she was very smart, very hardworking, but also headstrong and naive. After her recalcitrant reactions to Dr. Todd, the licensing board, and everyone else – she was shocked that no one budged from their positions at all. Her medical staff privileges were still suspended, and so was her medical license. She had lost her livelihood, which was her life. She wanted it back.

I still wasn't sure what Diane wanted me to do, exactly. I was sympathetic to her plight. *My* impression was that things had gotten out of hand in Charleston, which was understandable – strange city (Charleston, which she left long ago), strange setting (not her hospital), strange circumstances (death of her mother) – anyone might go a little crazy. At Ivory I did my third-year medical school rotations with her, and eight other students, and we shared some pretty intense situations – overwork, long hours, sleep deprivation – and I never got a hint that she was crazy. As far as I could tell, I was a heck of a lot more unbalanced than she was.

Based on that, and what I had observed at Excel McClain Hospital, I thought she was a good doctor and needed to start seeing patients again. I finished reading the packet at home on a Sunday afternoon. I phoned her to see what I could do to help.

"You are too naive," I said.

"What do you mean?"

I had the packet in front of me, thumbing through it. I said, "You see, these people in these impaired physician programs and on the licensing board have problems of their own. A real doctor, taking care of patients, like you and me, with real jobs – we don't have time to mess with this crap. So, if they can make you believe that you have a similar problem, or if they can get others to believe you have such a problem, it makes their lives easier to bear. You see?"

"My biggest mistake was trusting my lawyer."

"Right. A lawyer will not take care of you. Only you can take care of you."

"He didn't do his job."

"Did you ever see the psychiatrist, the one the licensing board and Dr. Todd wanted you to see?"

"Yes. She said I talked too fast."

I could believe that. Diane was talking too fast now. I said, "At this point, I think you need to go along with the program. Confess your 'sins.' Do your time. Then move on with your life."

"I didn't do anything wrong."

"*Of course* you didn't do anything wrong. What has that got to do with anything? Don't you see – they're holding all the cards."

"It's not fair. It's not right."

"So what?"

"So what?! If it happened to me, it could happen to anyone, it could happen to you."

"It already has."

"What do you mean?"

"I don't want to get into the details, it's too long a story, but I got sued for malpractice for five million dollars, and I only had one million dollars of malpractice insurance. If I lost, the judgment would wipe me out, and I would be trying to pay off the debt for the rest of my life. I'd be an indentured servant. So, for four years that lawsuit hung over me until the case went to a jury trial. Luckily, I won, but I could have lost. The details are different, but the concept is the same. It's not fair. Nobody cares."

"I've never been sued," said Diane.

"Then you've been lucky," I said.

Diane started talking faster: "Doctors get sued when you don't establish good relationships with your patients; you get sued when patients don't like you, or when they are angry, or a doctor screws up…"

"Stop!" I said. "A doctor can get sued at any time for anything, period, and it could happen to you, and you are correct, what is happening to you could happen to me. So I want to help. What do you want me to do, now?"

Diane said, "I just finished a book written by an attorney called *Winning*; it tells you how to get what you want."

"What do you want me to do, now?" I repeated.

"The first step is to get my medical license back. I want you to write a letter of support to the State Board of Medical Examiners. Their address is in the packet."

I finally knew what she wanted me to do. "Okay," I said, and we finished the call.

Sarah, my wife, heard some of the conversation. She asked, "Who was that?"

I told her.

"How's she doing?" asked Sarah.

"Not too good," I said.

"What happened?"

I told her.

When I finished, Sarah asked, "What does she want you to do?"

"She wants me to write a letter."

"Are you going to do it?"

"Yes."

I wrote the letter and sent it to the state licensing board and mailed Diane a copy. In it I said that I had worked with Dr. Murtaugh for many years, going all the way back to when we were medical students together at Ivory Medical School. I said I was familiar with her work with patients and that I had no doubts about her competence, integrity, and ethics – and that I thought it was in the best interests of the patients and the citizens of Tennessee that she be allowed to practice medicine.

Why did I do it? Obviously Dr. Murtaugh was a troubled woman, maybe even impaired, so why get involved? Two reasons:

1. Friendship.
2. I really thought she was a good doctor, and her patients were well served by her.

I had no idea whether the letter would do any good.

A couple of weeks later I was in my office, looking through my microscope, and I got another call from Dr. Murtaugh.

"I need your help again," she said.

"Okay."

"I just got a letter from a person named Mark Crofford, in the Office of the General Counsel for the Medical Licensing Board."

"I guess he's a lawyer."

"Yes. He wants to meet with me about my appeal. I have a meeting with him next Thursday afternoon at 4 p.m. I've learned never to go to one of these meetings alone. Will you come with me?"

"What do you want me to do?"

"Just be a witness."

"Okay."

The difference between the sublime and the ridiculous is about a millimeter, or less.

A year earlier, Dr. Diane Murtaugh's picture was on the cover of the Tennessee state medical journal as Physician of the Year, the most honored doctor in the whole state. The article in the magazine about Dr. Murtaugh was a six-page hagiography extolling her virtues as a physician and a person. It detailed how she graduated "with honors" from Ivory Medical School and then spurned more lucrative physician specialties to be a general practice pediatrician in Siegeburg. The article included numerous testimonials from her patients and colleagues extolling her medical expertise and her character. To summarize the article: Dr. Murtaugh was everything a physician should be – a credit to the profession.

Now, less than a year later, she'd lost her medical license and her hospital privileges, with all the disgrace, shame, and embarrassment associated with that. Diane told me, "This has been a poison to me."

That's how fickle fame and fortune can be, and I never forget it. I pray a lot.

Diane came to my office about 2 p.m. on the Thursday afternoon we were to meet with the lawyer. She came early so that we could go over her plan for the meeting. I hadn't seen her since this bizarre episode began, and I was struck by her appearance. She had lost a lot of weight, which was not a good look for her because she was thin and pale to begin with. Now her skin was so white and delicate that a few light blue blood vessels were apparent on the cheeks of her fair face, which had more wrinkles than a woman in her early forties should have.

Diane was still obsessed with the book *Winning*. She told me, "It says that you have to have a goal for each meeting, and I have three goals for this meeting. First, I want to look forward and not behind. Second, there does not need to be another hearing, that I should be reinstated because there was no evidence of harm to any of my patients, or any evidence of professional incompetence at all. And third, even if I have bipolar disorder, so what!? – you know what I'm saying." She was talking really fast.

"Right," I said very slowly.

Neither one of us talked much on the drive to downtown Nashville. The meeting was to be held in the William R. Snodgrass Tennessee Tower, a thirty-one-story building built in the style of a cube sticking out of the ground. To me it had the appearance of an architect's nightmare. As is usually the case when dealing with the government, trying to find a place to park was one of the biggest challenges. We were able to find a space on Charlotte Avenue. I put some money in the meter, and we walked the two blocks to the skyscraper.

Mr. Crofford worked on the tenth floor. We were a few minutes early, and the receptionist ushered us into a waiting area, a rectangular room with folding chairs next to each wall. That was it – no coffee, magazines, newspapers, windows – nothing. The receptionist left, and the two of us sat on our chairs and waited.

It was a short wait. After a couple of minutes, Mr. Mark Crofford entered the waiting area and introduced himself. He was a handsome African American gentleman, dressed in a dark suit, white shirt, and dark tie. He was about six feet three inches tall, lithe, and moved gracefully. "Handsome" doesn't really do justice to his appearance, which was charismatic, like a movie star, as handsome as Denzel Washington.

Mr. Crofford was cordial as we walked to his office, which was a mess – no desk, just a folding table with four matching folding chairs, enough to handle a bridge game. Mr. Crofford sat at the table; Diane and I picked out a couple of folding chairs and sat down. There were no windows. Filing cabinets were lined up like sentries against the four walls. The drawers of the filing cabinets were open, but there were no files in them. Instead manila files labeled "minutes of hearings," "interrogatories," "appeals," "briefs"…were bulging with documents and scattered around the filing cabinets, as if waiting to invade them. The walls were bare.

"You'll have to excuse the mess," said Mr. Crofford. "I'm just moving into this office and haven't unpacked yet. But I know you didn't want to put off this meeting. Dr. Murtaugh, what is it that you hope to accomplish today?"

Had he read *Winning* too?

And then Diane blew it. She began at the beginning, with what had happened at Charleston, which was fine, but she was talking too fast. And then she couldn't stop talking, and she talked nonstop for ten minutes.

Finally she concluded: "So right now patients are dying in Siegeburg, and I can't help them because I can't practice pediatrics anymore."

Mark Crofford said, "Obviously this is a very complex matter that could have been blown out of proportion."

"So what are you going to do about it?" said Diane.

"There's not a whole lot I can do," he answered. "You know the law as well as I do, and you must know at this point there is nothing I can do."

"Let me tell you about a patient…"

Mr. Crofford interrupted, "Mrs. Murtaugh…"

Diane interrupted, "I'm *Mrs.* Murtaugh nothing! I'm…"

"Sorry, *Dr.* Murtaugh, I didn't mean anything…"

"Listen!"

"Okay." Mr. Crofford leaned back in his chair, relaxed, listened.

Diane said, "Last weekend there was a two-year-old girl with a temperature of 102 degrees when she called me, I mean, when her mother called me." Diane was still talking too fast. She slowed down, a little. "I couldn't see the patient because I don't have a license. And Siegeburg was an underserved area when I moved there, and even now there's only one other pediatrician in town. The other pediatrician is swamped, because I can't help her, and by the time the other pediatrician was able to work the patient in and examine her, the patient's temperature was 104 degrees. This other pediatrician isn't very good at lumbar punctures, so she didn't do one, and sent the patient home on some antibiotics, but not the right ones, because she didn't get a culture of the spinal fluid, because she couldn't do a lumbar puncture. By the time the mother took her little girl to the emergency room, it was too late, and the child died of meningitis. I could have saved that little girl. Patients are *dying* because I don't have a medical license."

Mr. Crofford didn't say anything for a few beats. Then he looked at me. "Do you have anything to say?"

I said, "Just that I think Dr. Murtaugh needs to be seeing patients."

He turned to Dr. Murtaugh and said, "Dr. Murtaugh, the person keeping you from seeing patients is you."

She said, "I just want to get this stuff behind me."

"Then do it! Do what the board says — go see the psychiatrist the way you're supposed to." He shook his head. "I can't in good conscience suggest anything different, and my conscience means a lot to me these days. You see…"

"I don't want to hear it," said Diane.

"Listen!" he said.

Diane sat back, ready to listen. So did I.

"You see, I'm pretty much taking one day at a time, because I've got a six-year-old boy at home who lost his mother last year, when she died."

"How did your wife die, if you don't mind my asking?" I said.

"She had multiple myeloma."

"Tough," I said. "She must have been relatively young – shocking, tragic, that she suffered from that disease at such a young age."

"Actually, she was doing pretty well with the disease. She died during a simple operative procedure, a portacaval shunt."

Diane and I looked at each other in voiceless communication and questioning. A portacaval shunt is *not* a "simple procedure."

Mr. Crofford continued, "She had a reaction to the anesthetic and died for no good reason that I can tell." He looked directly at Diane. "So I'm all for putting the past behind me and getting on with life, you dig?"

On the car ride back to Siegeburg, Diane and I talked.

Diane said, "A producer in Hollywood has an option to make a movie of my life, about what happened."

"Did they pay you?"

"Yeah, but not much. It's a two-year option. I doubt if anything will come of it."

I expressed to her my interest in writing the screenplay. I fancied myself as a writer. I had a couple of screenplays out there, on the market. No one had expressed the slightest interest in either one of them – no plans to start filming a movie, no options, no money…nothing. No one had even bothered to steal my ideas.

So, with that in mind, I was interested in writing a screenplay about what had happened to Diane. My vision was that it would be a docudrama, maybe a made-for-TV movie. I proposed my ideas to her.

Diane was fine with that, wanted to collaborate on the project, with me writing the story and screenplay.

But that was the end of it. Later, when I reflected on the matter, I knew Diane Murtaugh and I would have creative differences, *big* creative differences. I suspected that her vision was that she took a hero's journey, a woman on a quest to defeat a bunch of men who tried to put a woman in her place – committing her to a psychiatric ward, stripping her of her hospital privileges, taking away her license to practice medicine, depriving her of a way to earn a living...and how she triumphed over these evildoers with a combination of pluck, courage, character, and intelligence – a movie with a heroine fighting a bunch of bad guys. That is the movie Diane would want to make.

Which would have been an okay story. However, as a screenwriter, I thought it would lack some elements of the typical hero's journey: change and transformation of the hero. The way I would write the screenplay is that the protagonist (Dr. Diane Murtaugh) would encounter complication after complication until she met the ultimate challenge, when she would have to a*dapt, change* and *transform.* Diane would never go along with that. She was not the one who needed to change. Everybody else did.

But even if Diane consented to letting me write the screenplay the way I wanted, I still think the project would have been doomed. I didn't really see Dr. Murtaugh's story as Manichean, with her as all good on one side, and her adversaries as all bad.

Instead, I saw her drama in shades of gray, like life, more of a novella, or short story, not a sweeping drama. At least some of the individuals opposing Diane seemed to me to be well-intentioned (Mr. Crofford, for example), even if I disagreed with some of their actions. And Dr. Murtaugh was not blameless in my opinion. I'm not a psychiatrist, but I really did think she was bipolar – and I should know. My father was bipolar, successfully treated with lithium, but bipolar all the same. He admitted his illness and got treatment. Dr. Murtaugh did not. She wasn't going to change – no hero's journey for her.

Diane's story never was written and produced. Instead what happened was this: on the drive back to Siegeburg, Diane asked me what she should do. This is what I said:

"Comply with what the board wants you to do. Fighting them...well...I just don't think you're going to win. Go see the psychiatrist, convince him or her that you are sane. Do whatever else they tell you to do; convince them that you are a good physician, that you can be trusted, that you can take care of your patients. You don't have to convince me. You have to convince the medical licensing board. Go along. I know this is like poison to you, but I don't see any other way."

I felt like I had said the same things before, to another impaired physician, Dr. Morris Benson, who listened. I thought possibly Dr. Murtaugh would listen as well. Maybe I was becoming an "impaired physician whisperer."

That night I had a dream:

I'm riding my motorcycle (something I haven't done since medical school) from Siegeburg to Nashville, speeding along Interstate 40. I'm on my way to Nashville's downtown area, to shop for clothes (I detest shopping for clothes). As I ride, I worry about where I am going to park my motorcycle, and I also worry about the weather — dark storm clouds are moving in from the west. So instead of reaching the downtown shopping area, I stop at a hotel where a medical school classmate of mine is staying, Brandon Walters. I ask Brandon to hold on to my billfold for me, which he agrees to do. I sit down and watch TV in the hotel room when Brandon's wife, who is a nurse, walks in. On the TV the talking heads are talking about the medical meeting to be held in Nashville that day, at the very hotel where I am staying. The nurse and I wonder if Dr. Schaeffer, the world-famous infectious disease specialist at Ivory Medical School, will attend and talk about the latest epidemic sweeping the country, whatever that is. I decide it's time to leave and go shopping for clothes, which is why I came to Nashville in the first place. I almost walk out without my wallet, but then I remember to ask Brandon to return it to me, which he does. It's a trifold wallet, which flips open to a compartment covered in plastic, which is where I keep my driver's license and the billfold copy of my medical license. They are gone. The compartment is empty. I go to the nearest desk and start taking out the contents of my billfold, frantically looking for my driver's license and medical license. Brandon and his wife help me look. I take everything out of the billfold — the money, the hotel key card, brochures to exotic tourist destinations, pamphlets about continuing medical education — so much stuff that it covers the entire desk; it's all there except for my driver's license and medical license, which must have slipped out and are lost somewhere. I finally give up and stop looking, and resign myself to spending time with the appropriate bureaucrats I need to see to get replacements. Then I wake up.

In real life, Dr. Murtaugh did get *her* medical license back. After our visit with Mr. Crofford, she did follow through with meetings with the psychiatrist approved by the Board of Medical Examiners and Dr. Todd. This "independent" evaluation was in Diane's favor. Her medical license was reinstated, on probation, with the probation to be lifted when Dr. Murtaugh provided proof to the board of forty hours of continuing medical education. She had one year to do this. It took her one month. Her probation was then lifted, and Dr. Murtaugh had all the usual privileges of a medical license in the state of Tennessee. She did it. She put her troubles with the state behind her. She was done.

She was also done with Excel McClain Hospital, which didn't want her back anyway. Unfortunately, no hospital in Tennessee wanted her to be a physician on their medical staff. There were two reasons for this: First, her out-of-control behavior was not only in the National Practitioner Data Bank – it was public knowledge, and no hospital wanted to take the risk of potential problems. Second, because of her record, Dr. Murtaugh was unable to get malpractice insurance – no insurance company would write her a policy; thus any hospital that accepted Dr. Murtaugh on the medical staff would be totally alone in defending any malpractice lawsuit that might arise out of Dr. Murtaugh's actions. No hospital would take that risk.

Westbound Highway 70 as it leaves Siegeburg has a conspicuous sign that marks the *Trail of Tears.* It's a brown sign with white letters delivering a succinct message: "Trail of Tears, Original Route." The letters surround a white tear-shaped image in the center, which contains a similar message in brown letters: "Trail of Tears, National Historic Trail." A driver traveling west continues to intermittently see these signs on Highway 70 and other roads heading west. They are monuments to a path that extended from Siegeburg to Oklahoma, part of the Trail of Tears in the Southeastern United States, on which about one hundred thousand Native Americans were involuntarily removed from their homes and relocated to "Indian Territory" in Oklahoma during the period from 1830 to 1850.

Approximately a century and a half later, Dr. Murtaugh took that very same trail from Siegeburg to Tahlequah, Oklahoma, where she found work as a pediatrician at the Cherokee Nation Hospital. It was a good match: Cherokee Nation needed a qualified pediatrician, and Dr. Murtaugh was as qualified as they come. She's still there.

I had no contact with Diane for several decades. She stopped coming to our medical school reunions. Instead, she sent letters to the class president with updates about her life. The class president circulated the letters at the Saturday night class parties, for everyone to read. I kept hoping that she would come herself, but that was not to be.

Then she showed up for our forty-year class reunion. Diane sat next to me at the banquet Friday night, and we talked some more at the class party on Saturday. She told me of the incredible things she had seen in her pediatric practice at Cherokee Nation, and a lot of it was good – the culture, traditions, respect for nature and the land…but some of it was bad – the alcoholism, abuse, and violence; one of her young patients, a boy, had watched both his parents get shot and killed. Diane shook her head with emotion.

But for Diane Murtaugh, M.D., the important thing was that she was needed and wanted, and that her patients and their families appreciated the care she provided. She seemed content, even happy.

And she didn't talk too fast anymore.

JUST FRIENDS

August 27, 1999

We're headed to a Titans football game, *the* place to be in Nashville on a Friday evening in late August. Although only an exhibition game, this will be the first game played in the brand-new Adelphia Coliseum and will showcase the city to the world.

Nashville is a small city that wants to be a big city. It has been a magnet for songwriters and musicians for decades, hence the moniker Music City, USA. But Nashville wants to be more than that. It wants to be chic, cool, and envied like San Francisco, Atlanta, Vienna, and Paris. City leaders want *Travel and Leisure Magazine, Conde Nast Traveler*, and every other travel magazine writing cover stories that describe Nashville as a destination city – and articles in *Business Week, Fortune*, and *Forbes* extolling this Tennessee city as a wonderful place to do business. Nashville's movers and shakers want growth, and lots of it, with new skyscrapers, a hot commercial real estate market, and rising home prices. Nashville wants it all, but most of all, Nashville wants money.

To that end Music City needs a National Football League team playing in a world-class stadium. That will happen tonight, and Nashville wants everyone to watch. The game has been hyped for weeks on print media, radio sports call-in shows, and television. ESPN will televise the game, not ESPN 2, but *the* ESPN. A bald eagle, a real one, will soar and start things off. Wow. Jeff Fisher, the Titans' coach, says, "This is the biggest game of my life."

Really? An *exhibition game*?

Well, I'll be there. I'm headed to the game with Bryan Magnuson, CEO of Excel McClain Hospital, and his sidekick, Kathy Lassiter, the chief operating officer. Excel Corp gave Bryan three tickets to the game. Of course he wanted Kathy to go, but rather surprisingly, he gave me the third ticket – maybe because I'm a hospital-based pathologist and therefore see Bryan and Kathy a lot. Most importantly, I'm not a real doctor who sees patients, and thus I have no clout, so Bryan and Kathy can relax and have fun with no pressure from me.

Kathy is single. Bryan is married, but his wife is not going to the game.

I'd never met Bryan's wife, and neither had anyone else at the hospital. I did know Bryan's two high-school-aged sons because they went to McClain Christian Academy, the same school my boys attended. From time to time I saw Bryan and his boys there – athletic contests, concerts, plays, and the like – but it was always just Bryan and his sons; Bryan's wife was never there. Nor was she ever at any hospital function; Bryan came alone. No one ever asked where his wife was, or even mentioned her. It was as if she didn't exist, or was hidden somewhere, like Mr. Rochester's insane wife in *Jane Eyre*. But this wasn't a novel, this was real life.

On the other hand, Kathy Lassiter and Bryan Magnuson were always together, as inseparable as Bob Hope and Bing Crosby in a "Road" picture. Bryan was CEO of the hospital, and Kathy was the chief operating officer, so Bryan was ostensibly Kathy's boss. But that wasn't the way it seemed – Kathy was the dominant one, and Bryan deferred to her.

Bryan was a relative newcomer to Siegeburg. He grew up in Kansas, went to Duke University, and then got an MBA from the University of Kansas. After his schooling, he started his career with some staff jobs at Excel Corp Headquarters, but his assignment at Excel McClain Hospital was his first real job.

In contrast, Kathy grew up in Siegeburg and received her nursing training close by at Tennessee Tech. With her RN degree, she started out in the emergency room at McClain Hospital and then became a nursing supervisor. After a few years she was promoted to director of Nursing. While working full-time she went to school part-time at Tennessee State University in Nashville and eventually got an MBA degree.

Shortly after Bryan came to Excel McClain Hospital, he made Kathy the chief operating officer, reporting only to Bryan. Kathy was unmarried and had no kids. Her job was her life. Excel McClain Hospital was her baby.

If I wanted anything done in the lab, or needed help in the pathology department, Kathy was the one to deal with, not Bryan. For example, if I needed a new microscope for the hematology lab, and asked Bryan for the funds to do that – his answer would be "Check with Kathy." Or, say I needed better lighting in the blood bank area; if I checked with Bryan about getting that done, similar answer –"I'll discuss it with Kathy."

And it wasn't just the lab that had this experience. If the operating rooms were getting too warm and needed a new air-conditioning unit to cool things down, nothing would get started until Kathy gave the okay. If the radiology department needed a new piece of equipment, Bryan needed to check with Kathy.

The same dynamic took place at the weekly management meetings. Bryan sat at the head of the table, supposedly in charge, with Kathy seated to his immediate left. The order of events for everything on the agenda was always the same: The item would be discussed by those with knowledge of the subject. Then Bryan would wrap things up. But nothing was ever final until Bryan turned to his left and said, "Kathy, is there anything you want to add?" or, "Kathy, is that pretty much the way you see it?"

The most common response of Kathy to Bryan was a demure smile and a nod, and it was on to the next item. But sometimes Kathy would express what she thought needed to be done, and Bryan would quickly fall in line. One hospital gossip said it best: "Bryan can't go to the bathroom without checking with Kathy."

We anticipate a crush of traffic near game time, so we get an early start. We meet at the Excel McClain Hospital parking lot four hours before kickoff. Kathy and Bryan arrive together in Bryan's car, a 1996 Chevy Monte Carlo. Bryan drives us from Siegeburg to Adelphia Stadium in Nashville. Kathy sits in the front, me in the back. There is minimal traffic, so we arrive at the stadium more than three hours before the start of the game.

The forecast is for clear skies. It's almost dusk, magic hour. On one side of the Cumberland River, the pristine Adelphia Coliseum shoots up to the sky like a silver and blue wonderland. On the other side of the river, the dusk sunlight reflects from the skyscrapers at an angle, so the Nashville city skyline shimmers and sparkles like gold and diamonds. The city seems to float above the river like the emerald city of Oz. That appearance will continue after the sun goes down because Mayor Bredesen has asked the businesses of downtown Nashville to leave their lights on so the city skyline will shine on national TV. What a vision: a brand-new lighted stadium on one side of the river, and the glowing Nashville skyline on the other.

Kathy was a quiet person, but when she did talk, she talked slowly, with gravitas, like her words were made of gold. Her questions tended to be hard to answer, and her comments tended to be hard to address.

For example, at one Executive Committee meeting, I was there along with the heads of the various departments of the medical staff, as well as the director of Nursing. An item for discussion/information was an edict from Excel Corporation's Investigational Review Board (IRB), which said that they had to approve any research done at Excel McClain Hospital.

Fair enough. But this was a change. As a kind of carryover from the time when Dr. Bob owned the hospital, there was kind of an "anything goes" attitude regarding publication of what we discovered in the course of taking care of our patients. For example, I had published a case report of a patient with HIV/AIDS presenting as MDS with thrombocytopenia. Other members of the medical staff had done similar writing. And as the bandits in *The Treasure of Sierra Madre* said, "We don't need no stinking badges," so did those of us on the medical staff say about our publications, "We don't need no stinking IRB."

Well, *now* we *did* need IRB approval, and nobody was happy about it, including Kathy. Bryan said, "Anything you want to add, Kathy?"

Kathy said, "How do they get the power to do this?"

Aaron Rickert, the hematologist-oncologist, said, "This is a change from how we are used to doing things."

"Yes, and how do they get the power to do this?" asked Kathy.

Steve Prescott, an internist, said, "They basically just said we have to do it."

"Who are 'they'?" said Kathy.

"The members of the IRB," said Steve.

"Who are the members of the IRB?" asked Kathy.

I said, "Most IRBs have a mixture of people, some in the medical field – nurses, a physician or two – as well as other individuals, maybe an ethicist, a clergyman, some laypeople…the usual suspects for this kind of thing."

Kathy said, "So they get to dictate what research gets done, what can be published?"

"Pretty much," I said.

"I still don't know how they get the power to do that," said Kathy.

"Things change," I said. "That's the legislation we have now. Of course, if you want to change the law back to the way it was – I don't know how to do that."

Which was where discussions with Kathy usually ended – someone saying "I don't know."

Bryan parks the car in our assigned area of the North End Parking Lot. We get out of the car and slowly walk all the way to the other end of the stadium, the South End Parking Lot, where Wilson Pickett will be giving a pre-game concert. The stadium and parking areas are huge, so it's a long walk. We are in no rush. It's a sunny 90 degrees on this late August afternoon. We're dressed in Titan colors – Kathy in navy blue dress shorts and a light blue blouse, and Bryan in cutoff blue jean shorts and a light blue golf shirt. I'm wearing navy blue cotton pants and a Titans jersey with the number 9 on it, Steve McNair's number.

As we walk, we soak in the festival-like atmosphere. Fans circulate around food stands with barbecue sandwiches, hot dogs, popcorn, beer, and sodas. It's Friday night, time to party. Young men check out the young women, and vice versa. Some older fans are tailgating, and the wonderful aroma of grilled hamburgers makes me hungry. We make a food stop, and we each get a hot dog – Kathy with a Diet Pepsi, Bryan with water, and me with a Coke. We eat standing up.

Of course the burning question all of us at the hospital had – doctors, nurses, staff, everybody – was: Do they…how can I put this…fornicate? Did they have sex? Were they lovers? Inquiring minds wanted to know.

It was a reasonable question. Kathy's office was next door to Bryan's, and it sure seemed like there were a lot of closed-door meetings between the two, either in Bryan's office or Kathy's. The two ate lunch together and always sat together at any meeting they attended. Kathy and Bryan were together the majority of their waking hours. But that's really not unusual. Many working people spend more awake time at the workplace than they do at home.

It's not surprising, then, that relationships at work mirror those of a family in some ways. An obvious one is that the boss-employee relationship can imitate a father-child relationship. In the case of Kathy and Bryan, the leadership roles they played at the hospital were kind of like the roles parents play in the home. The question was: Do they sleep together like Mommy and Daddy do?

Hard to tell. They did not look like a couple. Both Kathy and Bryan were okay in the looks department, but not great.

Kathy's strongest point was her figure. She was relatively tall, five feet eight, and her body went in and out in the right places. She was not thin, but did not have a weight problem at all. She was athletic – all muscle. Her idea of a good time on the weekends was to guide people on white water rafting trips down the Ocoee River, or go kayaking on her own. She was fit. The weakest part of her appearance was her facial complexion, which showed the scars of a losing battle with adolescent acne. She had long reddish brown hair, and her overall appearance was that of a Raggedy Ann doll, without the cute freckles.

Bryan was shorter than Kathy, about five feet six inches tall. He had sandy brown hair matched by a sandy brown goatee beard. Like Kathy, he was in great shape. He ran track and cross-country in high school and college and was really, really good – so good that when Bryan was in high school, he set the record for fastest time in the half mile *in the nation*. Bryan was still in good enough shape to run the Music City Marathon every few years.

Bottom line: They were both healthy enough for sex.

We finally make it to the South End Parking Lot of the stadium, where a simple stage is set up – a few steps leading up to a wooden platform with a gold-colored curtain as a backdrop. Wilson Pickett has not arrived yet. Instead, the stage is occupied by a band I've never heard of, singing songs I don't recognize, or like. We don't stay long. Instead we walk away and check out the vendors selling Titans T-shirts, pennants, and other paraphernalia. The sunlight bounces off the pavement, making everything hot and bright.

Ten minutes later we circle back to the concert area. By this time a crowd of several hundred fans has gathered, so we are unable to get very close to the stage. Nevertheless, we can't miss Wilson Pickett as he makes his entrance. He wears a shiny gold tuxedo with a black bow tie. His countenance and demeanor scintillate. Wilson Pickett shares a trait I've noticed in creative giants – like Peter, Paul and Mary, Simon and Garfunkel, and Paul McCartney. When they take the stage, they shine, glitter, and glisten like the stars they are. They appear immortal and not of this world.

Wilson Pickett sings "Mustang Sally" as he walks through the parking lot and then bounds onto the stage, flying more than walking. Soon everyone in the crowd claps and keeps the beat and rides along with "Mustang Sally" to the end of the song, when the crowd calms down a little, but not much. It's raucous, buzzing and shouting. Wilson Pickett introduces himself to the audience, which of course is unnecessary. We all know who he is. We're fans and show it with enthusiastic applause and yells.

Then something very interesting happens:

Wilson Pickett says, "Now all you men out there, any one of you who is with a good woman, raise your hands."

Hands shoot up all over the place. I do not raise my hand. I have a good woman, Sarah, my wife, but she's not "with me." She's home.

Will Bryan raise his hand? I glance in his direction. He does *not*.

Then Wilson Pickett says, "And now for all you ladies out there, any one of you who is with a good man, raise your hands."

Hands go up throughout the crowd. I watch out of the corner of my eye to see what Kathy does. She does nothing.

I feel like a chaperone.

Wilson Pickett proceeds to sing "In the Midnight Hour." I know the lyrics pretty well. I *will* wait 'til the midnight hour, and I *will* see if any "love comes tumbling down."

What we at the hospital wanted to know was this: Did the two of them, Kathy and Bryan, have sex with each other?

No one had any hard evidence that they did, but that didn't rule it out. I mean, let's face it – Bryan was the CEO of the hospital, and Kathy was the COO – they were the two most powerful people at the institution. No one was going to ask them directly whether they had sex with each other or confront them about it. Impertinent questions like that were not only rude, they could shorten your career. No one was going to spy on them — it wasn't that important. And if Kathy and Bryan were lovers, they were covering their tracks pretty well. To my knowledge, no one had any direct observation of any extramarital hanky-panky — no one had caught them in flagrante delicto or furtively entering and leaving a motel room together.

I had no direct evidence whatsoever that Bryan and Kathy were more than co-workers and friends. But I did have circumstantial evidence that they were lovers. There was this time Kathy, Bryan, and the hospital board members, including me, went to San Francisco for a retreat, ostensibly to attend a continuing education course on hospital management and governance. The real purpose of the trip was to reward the board members and senior management of the hospital with a vacation to San Francisco paid for by Excel Corp. Anyway, one day, one *whole* day, none of us saw Kathy or Bryan. They missed all the lectures, breakout sessions, coffee breaks, meals…both were as absent as Bryan's wife, nowhere to be seen.

Kathy and Bryan showed up the next day as if nothing had happened. At breakfast I asked Bryan, "How was your day yesterday?"

Bryan said, "Great. I went jogging, went to Fisherman's Wharf and back — loved going up and down these hills — sorry to miss the course yesterday. I just needed a break."

Later in the day I asked the same question of Kathy. She answered, "My day was fine. I spent it in my room, catching up on sleep."

Hmmmm.

And then there was this incident I observed at the Annual Excel McClain Hospital Christmas Dinner/Party. Kathy and Bryan sat at the same table. Bryan was super attentive to Kathy's needs that evening — holding Kathy's chair for her as she sat down or stood up, keeping her plied with drinks as needed, meeting her eyes whenever possible — typical seductive stuff. Near the end of the event, Kathy and Bryan finally danced together; it was a slow dance, and Bryan wanted to dance close to Kathy, in a romantic fashion. But Kathy did her best to keep him at a distance. I was not sure what was Kathy's motive in doing this. Was she just not into him that much, so she discouraged his advances? Or was she in fact Bryan's lover, but she wanted to be discreet and not flaunt it?

After the brief but enjoyable Wilson Pickett concert, we finally enter the spanking new Adelphia Stadium. It's spotless, like a new car. Bryan buys a round of beers for us, and we take our seats. We're on the thirty-yard line, about thirty rows up – good seats. Kathy sits between Bryan and me. We are still early, about an hour and a half till game time. Only a few fans have arrived. As time goes on other fans drift in. Most ask us, "Have they had the bald eagle yet?" We answer, "Not yet, you haven't missed a thing."

So Kathy did not want to dance close to Bryan. But she obviously cared a lot about him. About a year ago, on a Monday, Kathy came in to my office, obviously upset. "I'm worried about Bryan," she said.

I asked why.

Kathy said, "He was watching his son play in the band at a football game Friday night, and he collapsed."

"How do you know this?" I asked. I was at the game and hadn't seen a thing.

"He called me Friday night. But I know he was sick all last week. He didn't want anyone to know. Bryan doesn't want anyone to know what happened Friday night either."

Bryan walked by my office, making his morning rounds, but he must not have seen us because he didn't come in.

"I'm going to go get him," said Kathy.

Kathy came back in a few minutes, Bryan in tow. Bryan was carrying sheets of paper with him.

Bryan said," I did see a doctor last week, and he ran these tests." He handed me the paperwork.

"Who was the doctor?" I asked.

"Steve Prescott."

"Good choice."

"I've been so healthy all my life; it was a real change for me to have to find a doctor, because I've never needed one."

I looked over the data. I said, "Your thyroid tests are elevated. As you know, we don't have an endocrinologist here. Do you want me to hook you up with a big-city endocrinologist in Nashville, one I know is good?"

"Sure."

So I did. I phoned my old med school roommate, Jim Puckett, best man at my wedding, who was now an endocrinologist, and a good one. He was not taking new patients, but as a favor to me, he agreed to see Bryan.

Bryan and Jim hit it off. It turned out Bryan had a mild case of hyperthyroidism, easy enough for Jim to treat, and Bryan felt better. He wasn't cured though. Bryan was happy with Jim and the way Jim took care of him, but Bryan wasn't happy with something being wrong with him. "Just one more thing to make me feel older," he said.

My medical opinion was that nothing would make him feel younger than sex with Kathy Lassiter.

Faith Hill sings the national anthem, accompanied by the Nashville Symphony Orchestra. The performance is flawless, so perfect that Kathy thinks it was prerecorded and played over the sound system. I disagree. These are really talented musicians – this *is* Music City after all, where we take great music for granted.

At the conclusion of the music, a bald eagle flies from the top of the stadium to the grassy field at breathtaking speed, a blur of black and white. The crowd cheers.

The two teams – the Atlanta Falcons and our beloved Tennessee Titans – take the field. Football games take us back to adolescence – the running around, the music, the bright colors of the uniforms contrasting with the green grass of the field, and the sounds of the crowd – it's all so intense, like that time around puberty. Then there's the overt sexuality of the participants. The big, muscular, masculine football players wearing padded shoulders and tight pants run through and around formations of nubile cheerleaders with short dresses, bare midriffs, and accentuated busts. Put that altogether with the savagery of the game itself, and you have a hot mix of violence and sex – America's game.

Michael Buffer, the "let's get ready to rumble" guy, comes to the microphone. He says what he has been paid a lot of money to say: "Let's get ready to RUUUMBLE!" with his stentorian voice.

The game starts.

After the kickoff, the Titans have the ball. The first play is a long pass from Steve McNair to Frank Wycheck, our tight end. It's a completion, a back shoulder throw and catch – virtually impossible to defend when done right. Everyone cheers. After that though, it quickly becomes apparent that this is a game the fans (including me) don't really care about. In spite of all the hype, it's an *exhibition* game, a glorified practice. Also, no one really cares whether or not we beat the Atlanta Falcons. They are not a rival, just another team. My mind wanders, and I lose track of time. The bright stadium lights are on at the start of the game, scarcely visible, but then become more apparent as day merges imperceptibly into night. Then the coliseum glows like a well-lit cruise ship sailing across a dark sea at night.

One of the things I like about Kathy is that she understands football. She asks me why the yard markers are messed up, and I say I don't know; she asks this *before* the game is temporarily stopped to straighten out those messed-up markers. Once the game resumes, a backup running back gets tackled at the line of scrimmage for no gain, and she asks me, "Why are we going with all this inside stuff?" I have no idea. Good question though.

Just as the infantry marches on its stomach, so a football crowd needs to tank up with food and drink. By halftime the three of us are hungry, and we buy popcorn and soft drinks.

After half time, the starters are on the bench, not on the field, and what little interest we had in the game is over. Talk turns to affairs of the hospital. Peter White, the regional vice president of Excel Corp, is coming for a visit, for undisclosed reasons – just a routine visit to check up on things, as far as Kathy knows. Mr. White does want to meet with the medical staff Executive Committee, and the board of the hospital. I'm a member of both groups, and Kathy asks me to make reservations at a local restaurant for an evening meal to end his day. I suggest Morton's Steakhouse, which is fine with Kathy and Bryan.

The Titans win the game 17 to 9. The victory is celebrated by fireworks, which we want to watch. None of us has to work the next day, and we are in no hurry to leave. We walk to the top of the stadium to better see the fireworks, which beats getting caught in the pedestrian traffic of fans crowding the exits, and the jam of cars leaving the parking lots.

Plus, I love fireworks – have since I was a kid. I guess I'm still a kid. I like the rockets that explode into long strands of gold dust, and the ones that turn into blue sparkles. I like the explosions that set off three or four more explosions, each of which sets off three more in a chain reaction, which lights up the sky. I hear oohs and aahs from the crowd. A little boy about five years old stands to my right, and he is not sure about this fireworks stuff. He smiles at some of the fireworks, but frowns at others. Some of the louder explosions draw looks from him that say "I don't know about this." Finally the lad draws back and buries his head in his father's abdomen. He's had enough. His dad carries him gently away.

When the fireworks are over, we slowly make our way down the stadium steps and concourses to the nearest exit. We come out of the gateway to the parking lots. Our strategy of taking our time has worked – the crowd has thinned out, so it's a quiet and peaceful walk to Bryan's car. We three exist in a respite from work and family – relaxed and content.

Across the Cumberland River, the lights of the city are still on, and the Nashville skyline blazes away–symbolizing a Chamber of Commerce dream come true – an NFL football team playing on a beautiful night in a beautiful city.

"Mayor Bredesen is having a great night," I say.

Kathy and Bryan nod in agreement. The sky is a black canopy dotted with bright stars, but no clouds. A full orange harvest moon beams at us just above the horizon, straight ahead as we walk.

It's time for me to leave.

"I'll meet you at the car," I say and walk rapidly ahead.

Kathy and Bryan continue walking behind me at a languid pace. The Wilson Pickett concert, pregame festivities, football game, and fireworks are over. It's midnight.

Bryan and Kathy drift away from me, toward the river, to get a better look. The dark banks and black water contrast with the glittering Nashville city rising on the other side, a short distance away, just out of reach, like a dream. They walk closer to the river and closer to each other – then hold hands – forgetting about me and everything else. They turn to each other and kiss.

ON CALL

October 2000

At the monthly Internal Medicine Department meeting, physicians from two cardiology groups were fighting over patients, specifically how to allocate patients who came to the emergency room and needed a heart doctor. The motive for the dispute was simple: whoever took care of the patient got the money.

There were thirty of us in the conference room, which had the appearance of a classroom, with tiered seating, three tiers total, facing a blackboard. We were seated on uncomfortable folding chairs spaced out on each tier. The department chair, Dr. Aaron Rickert, sat in front of the blackboard, facing the members of the department, frowning, like a professor addressing a group of not very smart graduate students.

Aaron graduated from Massachusetts Institute of Technology, went to medical school at Harvard, and then did Internal Medicine/Oncology/Hematology training at Washington University Hospital in St. Louis – impressive. Once I asked him: Why was he at Excel McClain Hospital in Siegeburg, Tennessee – a small hospital in a small town in Tennessee – instead of at a major medical center, trying to win the Nobel Prize in Medicine?

His answer: "I didn't like all the political stuff in the big city."

I was not an official member of the Internal Medicine Department. I was a pathologist and a member of the surgery department, where I felt more at home. I like surgical-type diseases that I can see, touch, and feel – acute appendicitis, lung abscesses, skin cancer, brain tumors, and the like – diseases that demonstrate courage, attack patients head-on, and don't mess around. I don't like internal-medicine-type diseases – diabetes, hypertension, kidney failure – that seem to me to be abstractions that sneak up on a patient in a cowardly way but with severe consequences, even death. I fit in with surgeons better than internists.

But I had to attend the Internal Medicine Department meetings as an ex-officio member. The internal medicine docs wanted a pathologist there to answer any questions they might have about the lab. Also, if something went wrong, they wanted someone to complain to.

Internists tend to be a crabby bunch. I think it's because deep down they know they don't accomplish all that much. I mean, it is infrequent that an internal medicine doc "cures" a patient's disease. An internist can *treat* diseases like heart failure, cirrhosis of the liver, kidney disease, and dementia – maybe even make the patient a little better for a while – but *cure* the patient? Doesn't happen very often.

Everyone in attendance was bored because the agenda of the meetings typically was a review of things that had already happened, and approval of decisions that had already been made – not scintillating stuff.

So everyone was barely paying attention when Dr. Eduardo Escobar made a motion that "only physicians who actually work here be allowed to take call in the emergency room."

Everyone was half asleep, so there was no response for a few beats. Then Dr. Steve Prescott said, "This motion is based on greed, pure and simple, not patient care."

Everybody woke up. A discussion about who was on call was boring. But greed, now that was interesting.

"How so?" asked Dr. Rickert.

Steve said, "This is an effort by one cardiology group, Dr. Waldo's group, to limit the call opportunities of a competing cardiology group. I didn't know this was going to be on the agenda. It just showed up! I think this is too important a matter to be handled in such a capricious manner. I move we defer this item of business to the next meeting."

Aaron shook his head and then said, "Whatever this is, it's not capricious. I have agonized over this for a long time."

I hadn't been agonizing over this for a long time, but did know about the issue, which was: What was a fair way to allocate the patients who came to the emergency room with cardiac problems? The "right"

125

answer was not that straightforward, in my opinion. Here is a brief history of how this dispute came about:

Once upon a time there were two cardiology groups, both with competent cardiologists ready and willing to take care of patients who came to the Excel McClain Hospital emergency room with cardiac problems:

1. The McClain Cardiology Group had been there the longest, the first cardiology group at the hospital decades earlier, and until recently, the *only* cardiology group around. The three cardiologists in this group worked exclusively at Excel McClain Hospital. Even their office practice was based in a building leased from the hospital. They owned homes in Siegeburg and sent their kids to Siegeburg schools. The president of this group was Dr. Dennis Waldo.

2. The Christian Cardiology group was so named because it was based at Christian Hospital, a huge private hospital in downtown Nashville. The Christian Cardiology Group was composed of twelve cardiologists, and Dr. Greg Burckhardt was the newest member. He had joined the group after finishing his training at Ivory Hospital in Nashville. Dr. Burckhardt practiced at Christian Hospital of course, but several months ago started practicing at Excel McClain Hospital as well, the only member of his group to do so. He lived in Brentwood, a suburb of Nashville. It took him forty-five minutes to an hour to drive to Excel McClain Hospital when he had a patient to take care of.

Dr. Burckhardt had joined the medical staff at Excel McClain Hospital in hopes of getting more patients and more work. With eleven other cardiologists in his group, Dr. Burckhardt had trouble growing his Christian Hospital–based practice. It was hard to find his niche.

However, the three cardiologists in Dr. Waldo's group already at Excel McClain Hospital, and already living in Siegeburg, did not appreciate having another cardiologist around – they didn't need the help, thank you very much. But there really wasn't anything they could do to prevent Dr. Burckhardt from providing his services to the hospital and the Siegeburg community. Dr. Burckhardt was a well-educated, well-trained cardiologist. So he became an active member of the medical staff, and there were four cardiologists on the Excel McClain medical staff – three from Dr. Waldo's group, and Dr. Burckhardt.

Dr. Burckhardt's practice grew slowly but consistently. He was a good doctor and took good care of his patients. His income went up. He was able to contribute his share to the overhead of his group. He also helped out Excel McClain Hospital. Not only did he help take care of the cardiology needs of the Excel McClain Hospital patients, but his work generated payments to the hospital. Every time he ordered X-rays, cardiac rehab services, lab work, treadmill studies and other billable procedures to help take care of his patients, the hospital was able to generate revenue: ka-ching, ka-ching.

Dr. Burckhardt contributed in other ways as well. He did his share of unreimbursed service work to the hospital, like serving on the pharmacy committee and infection control committee, which was boring uncompensated work, but needed for the hospital to function. He also helped review medical charts for the Quality Assurance Committee, which was mind-numbing but necessary.

Dr. Burckhardt also took emergency room call. With four cardiologists on staff, and one cardiologist needed for call each twenty-four-hour period, Dr. Burckhardt ended up on call every fourth day. And the income derived from seeing a patient in the emergency room wasn't just the ER patient consult. Usually there would be follow-up needed as well – coronary arteriography, pacemaker placement, office visits…which would be done by the cardiologist who made first contact in the ER. Those services were lucrative. There was a lot of money in cardiology, money worth fighting over.

That call schedule worked out okay, not great, but okay. In fact, I suspected Dr. Waldo's group kind of liked the help; when Dr. Burckhardt took cardiology call in the ER, that was one less day that Dr. Waldo's group had to cover, which meant more time off. A little less call meant a little less money, but the extra time off was nice. Excel McClain Hospital was happy with Dr. Burckhardt. Dr. Burckhardt was happy with his growing cardiology practice. Even Dr. Burckhardt's group was sort of happy with the additional time off. Everyone got along.

Until things changed. Dr. Burckhardt's group came up with a simple but brazen scheme to build up his practice even faster: All the other cardiologists in the Christian Hospital Cardiology Group applied for medical staff privileges at Excel McClain Hospital, all *eleven* of them. And Dr. Burckhardt, as well as the eleven additional cardiologists in his group, would all take call for the emergency room – twelve cardiologists total.

That meant there would be a total of fifteen cardiologists on staff (three from Dr. Waldo's group and twelve from the Christian Hospital Group), each one taking call in the emergency room. Doing the math, the result was that the Christian Cardiology Group went from covering one out of four days (25% of call), to twelve out of fifteen days of call, or 80% of the available call, which translated into 80% of the money. That was a significant jump in market share – 25% to 80%! Coca-Cola could only dream about taking that kind of market share from Pepsi.

The other part of the Christian Cardiology scheme was that all the patients seen in the ER by the Christian Cardiology Group were sent to Dr. Burckhardt for follow-up care and treatment.

Finally, the Christian Cardiology Group added yet another way to increase Dr. Burckhardt's practice. Whenever someone from Dr. Burckhardt's group was called by the ER to see a cardiac patient, that cardiologist didn't come to the ER, but instead contacted Dr. Burckhardt, who came to the Excel McClain Emergency Room, and took over the care of the patient.

These measures worked as intended. Dr. Burckhardt's practice grew. At the rate he was building his practice, he would soon be a very busy and very rich cardiologist, which was good for him.

Not so good for Dr. Waldo's group though. Dr. Waldo and his partners could maybe live with one extra cardiologist, Dr. Burckhardt, taking call, but *twelve* – that was too much. Dr. Waldo regarded what Dr. Burckhardt's group was doing as an escalation and an existential threat to his McClain Cardiology Group. What to do about it though? That was tricky.

First, Dr. Waldo tried a direct frontal attack. A few weeks before the Internal Medicine Department meeting, Dr. Waldo confronted Dr. Frank Moneypenny, the emergency room medical director, who, as a hospital-based physician, had no real power. Therefore Dr. Waldo thought he could coerce Dr. Moneypenny into helping him. It was an unpleasant conversation.

Frank told me about it: "Dr. Waldo wanted me to ignore the ER call schedule and ignore the members of Dr. Burckhardt's group, and just make sure that Dr. Waldo's group got most of the ER's cardiology patients, as was the case before Dr. Burckhardt came on the scene. I refused to do that. The conversation grew heated."

"I always thought Dennis Waldo was kind of a low-key guy," I said.

"I saw a side of Dennis I never saw before," said Frank.

Frank stood his ground.

Dr. Waldo couldn't think of any other direct way to address the issue and change the call schedule. He knew that it would be difficult to get support from others at the hospital regarding this issue for two reasons:

1. Apathy. Most of the physicians had problems of their own, without worrying about cardiologists. In fact, if they thought about it at all, their thinking was the more cardiologists, the better. Competition was a good thing.
2. Some of the physicians liked Dr. Burckhardt better than Dr. Waldo and the other cardiologists in Dr. Waldo's group.

This story is about war and politics, on a small scale perhaps, but conflict just the same. So, in this drama about conflict, who are the good guys, and who are the bad guys? Which cardiology group represents the dark side, and which cardiology group represents the good? Who are the heroes of this story?

Beats me.

This is one of the things that makes life so hard, at least for me. I struggle, I really do, to figure out what is right and what is wrong. Is it just me? Or does everyone feel this way, at least from time to time. Take this issue, which cardiology group was in the right?

Perhaps Dr. Burckhardt and his group were doing good. You could make a case that it's a free country, and that if Dr. Burckhardt's group wants to expand to Siegeburg, then who am I, who is anybody, to stop them?

But Dr. Waldo's group had a case to make as well. After all, the members of that group were already there, for heaven's sake, serving the community and doing a good job of it, by the way. Who did this other group think they were, moving in and taking over? It was as if a Walmart opened up in Siegeburg and put the local hardware stores out of business.

Dr. Waldo thought what was happening to him and his group was wrong, and he thought there was a case to be made to prove that. But a direct frontal attack didn't work, and wouldn't work, because it would seem selfish and self-serving. He needed an ally to make his case, that what Dr. Burckhardt's group was doing was wrong.

Finding an ally wasn't all that easy, because in essence this was a political issue, not a patient-care issue, and physicians tend to either not care about politics, or be naive about politics. Also, getting involved in this matter meant conflict, and physicians hate conflict. Finally, involvement in politics does not generate income; a physician generates income by taking care of patients, not spending time on political fights.

Dr. Waldo needed someone to make his case for him at the Internal Medicine Department, a physician who *did* regard politics as important. There weren't many. There was one, though, and that person was Dr. Eduardo Escobar.

Dr. Escobar learned the hard way that political matters are important, about as important as anything. He was born and raised in Cuba and became a physician. He was not interested in politics and cared only about his patients. He did not care about who was in power (Fulgencio Batista) and who was out of power (Fidel Castro), and didn't care who won in the struggle between these two for power. It didn't matter to him…until it did. Castro prevailed, and those who were not fervent supporters of the Revolution had to get out of the country, pronto. Eduardo and his wife and one other physician named Maria Perez made it to a small getaway boat and headed for the USA. The police tried to stop them and fired guns at the fleeing boat. Eduardo's wife was shot and killed. Eduardo and Maria made it to America. The two of them eventually married and settled in Siegeburg; Eduardo practiced internal medicine, and Maria practiced psychiatry.

Eduardo Escobar and Dennis Waldo had worked together for a long time. Eduardo was a general internist, not a cardiologist, and Dennis had helped him take care of his patients' cardiac issues for decades. Eduardo trusted Dennis and was loyal to him. He was willing to help Dr. Waldo.

So Eduardo made a motion: "Only physicians who actually work here should be allowed to take call in the emergency room." This was what Dr. Waldo wanted to happen.

And Steve's comment was that limiting call was "based on greed pure and simple, not patient care," which advocated for the position of Dr. Burckhardt.

Dr. Waldo sat in the back row and didn't say anything. Dr. Burckhardt wasn't there. This would be war by proxy.

Eduardo responded: "This is 'fronting' plain and simple. When someone from Dr. Burckhardt's group gets a consult, he doesn't show up. Instead Dr. Burckhardt shows up, even if someone else gets the phone call. Whoever takes the call contacts Dr. Burckhardt, and Dr. Burckhardt is the one who comes in, examines the patient, reads the EKG, looks at the lab work, and takes over the care of the patient. And then keeps taking care of the patient – doing the follow-ups in his office, doing the cardiac catheterization in Nashville, and doing whatever else needs to be done. Dr. Burckhardt is the only one in his group who actually sees patients here, no matter who is called. The rest of the cardiologists in his group are just figureheads fronting for him – it's not right."

Aaron Rickert shook his head. "Look, I don't have a dog in this fight. If you all want to limit cardiology call to who actually comes here, I'm okay with that. If you want a cardiologist to get all his friends and partners on the medical staff, who then takes over their patients, well, I'm okay with that too."

No one said anything for a few beats.

Kathy Lassiter, the hospital chief operating officer, said, "We're not talking about that many patients are we, ones who come into the ER who are unassigned, who don't already have a cardiologist?"

"Right," said Aaron as he shook his head again in frustration. "You would think that these are not enough patients to be fighting over, but I'm here to tell you *these two groups* are acting like they are fighting over gold."

A good point. This was not a Universe-Changing Event with the Future of Earth and Mankind hanging in the balance. Even on a smaller scale, there was no baby two women were fighting over, that Solomon had to threaten to divide. Nobody was going to die, no matter what the outcome. This wasn't even a patient-care issue – all the cardiologists were competent.

Still, the stakes were high enough – professional survival. It's a competitive world out there, and patients are the lifeblood of physicians – no patients, game over. These cardiologists had to support themselves and their families – who can't relate to that?

My mind raced through various solutions:

1. Let each member of the medical staff, regardless of group affiliation, rotate call. The larger the group, the more call that group gets. That's what was happening, and it was not working.

2. Rotate call by group rather than by individual cardiologist. In this case, two cardiology groups would share call equally, alternating nights and weekend call. That might have worked in this case, but this possible solution had ramifications. Do this for one specialty, and it had to be applied to all specialties – general surgery, orthopedics, pediatrics…The other departments would get dragged into this dispute, and they would not have liked that. That solution would not have worked.

3. The hospital could do what they do with hospital-based physicians – radiology, emergency room, anesthesiology, and pathology (my specialty) – which is write a contract with one of the cardiology groups to provide exclusive cardiology services to the hospital, just as the hospital does for these hospital-based services. I didn't think that would work though. Hospital-based physicians tend to have episodic encounters with patients as they come to the hospital – not repeated contacts that cardiologists have with their patients – in the ER, in their offices, at a treadmill fitness test, in the coronary catheterization suite…Also, there are efficiencies in equipment use, scheduling, staffing, administration and the like that are gained when one group has an exclusive contract to handle a hospital-based specialty. That would not be the case with a more patient-based specialty, like cardiology. That solution would not have worked either.

I agreed with Steve Prescott. This issue was too big, complicated, and complex to be decided by a large group of doctors at a department meeting.

I had an idea and spoke up: "Let's set a definition for members of 'active staff' who can take call, which would include objective numeric measures of what patient-doctor encounters are required to be 'active staff' – number of patient admissions, consults, procedures, or some other criteria – whatever each department comes up with. And the department could come up with a minimum number of patient contacts that defines a medical staff member as active; I don't know what that number is, maybe fifty, maybe more, maybe less – but whatever that number is, as long as the physician, in this case a cardiologist, meets those criteria, which apply equally to everyone, then that person can take call, regardless of what group he is in, or the size of his group, or anything else."

My comments were met with total silence. That meant whatever I said was really smart or really stupid.

Finally Aaron said, "I like Jack's idea. I think it addresses Dr. Escobar's issue of 'fronting.' All the members of Dr. Burckhardt's group would have to show up and take care of patients and do some work, at least enough to merit staying on the active medical staff. On the other hand, the standards would be applied equally to both groups."

Eduardo said, "I move we table my motion and let Aaron appoint a steering committee to explore this and report back to the Medicine Department. If they come up with something we can agree on, we can approve it and go from there."

Steve seconded the motion, which passed on a voice vote, with no dissent.

Aaron went on to the next item of business.

THE AFFAIR

August 2001

I was sitting near the end of a long table at Gretchen's Pizza, on a Friday night in August, following the annual Excel McClain Doctors versus Hospital Staff softball game. The aroma of beer and pizza pleasantly dominated my senses. Every athlete, no matter what the level of competition, has the game of his life, and I had just finished mine. I played shortstop on the Doctors' team, and the ball kept coming my way, and my glove was like a vacuum cleaner. In a seven-inning game, I must have had at least ten put-outs without a single error, and I went four for four at the plate. For the first time in years the Doctors' team won. The pizza tasted really good.

Rob Masterson, an obstetrician-gynecologist, sat on my left, and a bunch of other docs were sitting across from me, all men. We were still in our softball uniforms – shorts and blue T-shirts with the logo "Dazzling Docs." The chair to my right at the end of the table was empty.

Until Annie Layne, the operating room director, sat down next to me and turned slightly my way. She did not speak, but looked directly at me, with a *Mona Lisa* smile of charm and mystery. I thought: this is interesting.

I had noticed Ms. Layne before, as had every heterosexual male in the hospital. She was about five feet four inches tall, with coal black hair cut in a trim bouffant, which framed a clear countenance. Annie's outstanding feature, though, was her athletic figure – trim, firm, and muscular – remnants of her youth when she rode saddlebred horses competitively, winning many trophies. I was envious of the horses. But she was in her early forties and too old for that kind of competition. I was in my early fifties and too old for a lot of things.

"How do you like being OR director?" I asked. Annie had arrived at Excel McClain Hospital about ten years earlier, replacing Mary Ellen Masters, a woman who had been OR director for decades. Annie had transferred to the Siegeburg Excel McClain Hospital from a large Excel Hospital in downtown Nashville, where she had been the assistant director of the Operating Room Department.

"Great!" said Annie. "What an exciting time this is, with the growth of the hospital and the community. It was challenging though, at first, to take over for Miss Mary Ellen – she was an institution."

"You've been here a while though," I said. "I'd say you're an institution yourself."

She smiled and laughed and said, "Don't say that. It makes me sound so old."

We talked, but we didn't really talk; instead it was like the song "Some Enchanted Evening" playing in Gretchen's Pizza instead of at an officers' club dance in *South Pacific*. It wasn't what we said that made the evening magical. It was the way we said the words and the way we heard them – like we were the only two persons in the restaurant. Annie told me that she grew up in Ohio, but when her parents moved to Siegeburg, she moved to Siegeburg. Her family name was a prominent one in Siegeburg, not as ubiquitous as Dr. Bob's name perhaps, but the moniker "Layne" was prominent. Off the top of my head I could think of the Layne Drug Store, Layne Nursery, and Layne Funeral Home – all important places of business in Siegeburg. Annie lived with another woman, Meg, who was an OR nurse at a large hospital in Nashville, and Meg's grown son. The three shared a mortgage and living expenses.

Of course, I lived with another woman and her son also – that would be Sarah, my wife, and our third son, Richard, who was eleven years old. My two oldest boys, Eric and Matthew, were grown, long gone, and on their own. Sarah and Richard were not at Gretchen's Pizza and hadn't been at the game. Sarah had stopped coming to these events years ago, unlike earlier times when the boys were younger, and my whole family came to the games. Those were good times.

Annie asked, "Why did you go into pathology?"

"When I was a little boy, I loved science; I was one of those kids with a chemistry set that you ordered from a Sears Roebuck catalog. I made hydrogen sulfide that stunk up the house, tried to make a bomb or two. Luckily my dad was around and kept me from blowing up the house. I caught caterpillars, put them in a bottle with whatever they were eating, watched them make cocoons, and turn into butterflies and moths, which I let go. I was a rock hound – collected obsidian, shale, granite, and all those other stones you could collect in the fifties. So pathology, the science of disease, was a good fit for me."

Annie seemed interested.

"Why did you become an OR director?" I asked.

"I always wanted to be a nurse. And then I had this nursing school teacher in Ohio, who was an OR nurse, who must have had her eye on me, because she threw me into all these surgery rotations, and I was hooked."

And so was I.

The next few weeks I thought of little else but Annie. A few weeks later I asked her for a date. I knew she liked sports, so I asked her to go to a college football game, a pretty good one, between Tennessee and Alabama at Neyland Stadium.

My dear reader asks: Why?

And I answer: I don't know.

My dear reader asks: Why isn't it enough that you have a beautiful wife and three great boys?

And I answer: I don't know.

My dear reader asks: Who are you to want more?

And I answer: I know I'm a nobody and don't deserve what I have.

But at the time I didn't need to worry about any of that. Annie declined my invitation. She said, "I'm flattered, and the feeling is mutual, but you're married." Which was the answer I deserved.

Three years went by. Nothing happened, at least nothing romantic or sexual. I went to work and did my job. So did Annie.

We were around each other from time to time – meetings of the infection control committee, surgery department, quality assurance committee and the like. Often we walked past each other when I had to go to the operating room suite for an OR consult. Sometimes we had to work together on projects. For example, the hospital got inspected every three years by the Joint Commission on Accreditation of Hospitals; Annie and I worked together to make sure everything was in order with respect to the handling of surgical specimens, transfusion of blood products, and other areas where the OR and laboratory worked together.

We saw each other at other hospital-related events as well. Of course, each August there was the Annual Medical Staff versus Hospital Staff softball game, with pizza afterwards. Annie and I were there, and I noticed her, maybe she noticed me, but we didn't talk. What was there to say?

In addition each spring there was an Excel McClain–sponsored golf tournament at the Siegeburg Country Club. The hospital pretty much closed down for an afternoon, for a "four ball scramble" tournament. Each foursome had a mixture of good, average, and beginning golfers, and I was squarely in the average classification. At one tournament Rob Masterson and I were in the same foursome, and the two of us rode around in the golf cart, chasing our golf balls – a very scenic trip with a lot of fun. At the end of nine holes, Rob and I took a break and drank a beer on the clubhouse patio. Annie rode by in a golf cart driven by Tom Bruno, an orthopedic surgeon and former football player for the United States Military Academy at West Point. "I'm having a great time," Annie said to me and Rob as she drove past, smiling and laughing.

Those were prosperous years for my pathology practice and for Excel McClain Hospital. With growth came construction, and the Excel Corp added two new patient floors to the hospital tower, as well as a new operating room suite and laboratory. The lobby was also remodeled. There was a "topping out" party on a Thursday afternoon, with guided tours of the new facilities under construction. We wore hard hats during the walk arounds. Annie and I were both there, but not together. Annie spent most of her time with Peter White, the Excel regional vice president in charge of all the Excel hospitals in Tennessee, who showed up to make remarks and officiate the topping-out ceremony. Peter was a jovial roly-poly guy with a perpetual smart-ass grin on his face. Peter was obviously interested in Annie, not too interested in me. Was Annie interested in Peter, who was also married, by the way? I didn't dare ask.

I didn't dare ask Annie anything. For three years I thought about her a lot, not all the time, but a lot, but any follow-up romance between Annie and me? Nope. Nothing happened.

Until it did.

The venue was the open house for the hospital expansion on a Sunday afternoon in late February. Hundreds of Siegeburg citizens showed up and stood in the hospital lobby, waiting for the festivities to start. No one from my family was there. Everyone else was. Our politicians were well represented. The mayor of Siegeburg and our state senator attended. An ex United States senator was there, who also happened to be Excel Corp's CEO. Peter White was there, but Annie was standing next to me, not Peter White, or anybody else. At 1 p.m. Bryan Magnuson walked partway up the steps from the lobby to the second floor, turned to face the hundreds of citizens (and potential patients) down below and made some brief opening remarks. Annie stood close to me. She had to. It was crowded, and there wasn't much room. She didn't seem to mind. I sure didn't. After Bryan finished speaking, Peter White made a few remarks, and the Excel Corp CEO finished up. Everyone was excited.

After the speeches, I asked Annie if she wanted to see my new office, which was part of the new laboratory. She did. We walked from the lobby, around the corner, to my office a short distance away. Since the event was held on Sunday afternoon, the laboratory was quiet. Everything in the lab was new, shiny, and gleaming. There was magic in the air. I was dressed in my best black suit and red tie. Annie was dressed in a white blouse with gray stripes and a black skirt, which matched her black hair. She looked fantastic. I was excited. No one else wanted to see my new office, so no one else was around as we walked in the room. I closed the door and locked it.

"Oh," she said, and smiled.

I kissed her, and she kissed me back. My feelings were best expressed by "This Magic Moment" by Jay and the Americans – my feelings at the time, in symphony. She smiled and left.

I looked around our new lab for a while. About thirty minutes later I decided to check out the new operating room suite as well. Unlike my office or the lab, the operating room suite was crowded with visitors. How often does a patient get to tour the operating room facilities without being operated on? The Excel McClain Hospital OR was *the* place to be on this Sunday afternoon. I walked through the operating rooms, anesthesia area, patient holding areas, and break room. Everything was spacious, new, clean, and state of the art.

Annie saw me, and without a word, she led me to her office, closed the door, and locked it. We stood face-to-face in front of her desk. She kissed me. "You're special," she said.

Joy! Joy! Joy! Annie loved me. I walked on sunshine, air, and every other medium you can think of. When I commuted to work or anywhere, I listened to the music of my youth, sixties music, volume turned up. Whenever Percy Sledge's song "When a Man Loves a Woman" came on, I turned up the sound till it was almost deafening. It was a miracle I didn't get pulled over for disturbing the peace.

Annie visited me in my office, not every day, but some days. It was a good day when I saw her, and a bad day when I didn't. When she came to me, she sat across from me, on the other side of my desk and microscope, and we talked until most people went home, and we were alone. Then we closed the door and kissed. This went on for a few months.

The weekends were long, because I didn't see her. "How did you spend your weekend?" I asked.

"I went to the lake with Meg and her son. We went sailing. I tried to keep busy. I thought maybe that way I could stop thinking about you, but I didn't."

"I think about you all the time," I said.

The weekdays went by fast.

Annie was my soulmate. "What happens when we die?" she asked.

"No one knows," I said. "The unbeliever can talk a good game, and say 'nothing happens,' but at the back of his mind there is a hint of doubt, a whisper, like the breeze rustling the leaves of a tree, and he wonders – maybe I'm wrong. Similarly, the believer trusts in a heaven and glorious life after death, but even the most fervent believer too has doubts – maybe this life, *this*, is all there is. Think of 'doubting Thomas.' Even Jesus struggled in the Garden of Gethsemane. No one knows what happens when we die."

We talked like that.

Another conversation, more down to earth:

"Do you go to church?" I asked.

"Yes. Mainly for my parents' sake. They go, and I go with them when I can, when I'm not working."

"What church do you go to?" I asked.

Annie told me; it was the biggest protestant church in Siegeburg. She said, "It's hard for me to take the church too seriously. Many of our surgeons attend, and other doctors as well, and they are ushers and leaders of the church and all that, and they act so pious. Then when they're not at church, they do everything they can to get in my pants."

The Excel McClain golf tournament took place in early June. As usual it would be a four ball scramble. I asked Kathy Lassiter if she could pair me up with Annie Layne, and she said that she would.

Annie was a procrastinator and put off signing up for the event. Every day I asked her if she had signed up yet, and every day her answer was, "Not yet, but I will today." This went on for days and weeks, and it got pretty close to the deadline for signing up. It looked like I was going to be alone again.

The day of the deadline Annie phoned me from her office while I was looking at some slides. She was laughing. "I just got a call from Kathy Lassiter. She told me, and I'm quoting: 'Dr. Spenser, who is on the Board of Trust, wants you to be in his foursome at the golf tournament. So I'm signing you up. Be there."

I said, "I didn't know I had that kind of power."

Annie said, "I think people like you and me, we have that kind of power, but we don't know we have that kind of power."

A few days before the tournament, I went to the golf practice range to work on my swing. I was just a mediocre amateur golfer and did not want to embarrass myself. Annie said she was really looking forward to the golf tournament. She said she wanted to "consummate" our relationship. I hoped I could do *that* without any practice.

It was a hot humid Friday in early June at the Siegeburg Golf Club. Annie and I came in separate cars, but parked next to each other. It was close enough to Nurses' Day that a gift was not out of line. I gave her a coffee table book about horses – illustrated throughout with handsome riders and magnificent horses. Annie loved the book, and she loved me, and I loved her. What a day!

We walked to the clubhouse and paired up with the two other golfers in our foursome. One was Rob Masterson, the ob-gyn doc who had been sitting with me at the softball pizza party when all this started. Dr. Mitch Thornburg, a surgeon, was the final member of our group.

We headed to our golf carts.

Which turned out to be awkward.

Tom Bruno, the orthopedic surgeon, took it into his head that Annie should ride in his cart. He invited her to join him.

Annie pointed out the assignments had already been made.

Dr. Bruno didn't care. He would change the assignments.

I didn't think that was a very good idea.

Annie wouldn't budge, and neither would I.

Dr. Bruno finally accepted defeat, and not very gracefully.

Annie and I took our cart to our first hole with Rob and Mitch right behind us. Once on the tee, I hit a pretty good drive. I continued to play okay.

Annie was a great athlete, with no fat, and shapely muscular legs from all that horse riding. She looked great in shorts and a golf shirt. Nevertheless, she struggled at golf. This was only the second time Annie had been golfing, ever, and it showed. But that didn't make any difference – we had a great time, laughing, smiling, and cutting up on this gorgeous hot June day. After nine holes Annie and I were done with golf. At the clubhouse turn, we told Mitch and Bob to carry on, but we were through.

We had about four hours until the banquet that evening.

"I have a room," I said. "I hope that's okay."

"I was hopeful," she said.

What struck me was the quiet. We had privacy for the first time ever. We didn't have to talk in hushed tones so no one else could hear, or talk in code, worried about someone eavesdropping. No one interrupted us or interfered with us – just the two of us, together, what a blessing, what a gift on earth.

"Are you ready for this?" asked Annie.

I was.

We kissed and caressed, kissed and caressed, and made love.

"Having fun?" she asked.

I was.

We never made it to the banquet. Around 8 p.m. that night, Annie left the room, and then I left. On the way home, I stopped by the golf club and went to the hallway outside the dining room. Pictures of the golf foursomes were available for pickup, one copy for each member of the group. I looked at the picture, and the two of us looked very happy. I picked up two photos, one for me and one for Annie. On Monday I gave Annie one of the pictures, which she put on her desk. Anyone coming into her office saw a picture of me and Annie, together, looking like we were in love, because we were.

What followed was intense. A typical day went like this: We talked on the phone first thing in the morning. Then Annie got the operating room going, and I looked at microscopic slides. Sometimes I was interrupted by a surgeon needing an operating room consult, so I walked to an operating room. Sometimes Annie was scrubbed in on the case, and we would look at each other, both of us in scrubs and masks. When we got our work done, I would call her, or she would call me, and we talked. This happened several times a day. Sometimes after work Annie came to my office, and we necked like teenagers. On Sunday afternoons I often came into my office to get a head start on the week. This was nothing new – I had been doing this for years. What was new was that Annie would come to my office on those Sunday afternoons, and after my work was done, we talked and kissed. My office was in an alcove off to the side of the lab, behind a door that was locked at night and on weekends. We weren't totally private or comfortable, but at least we could see each other and share time, in a kind of sick but romantic way. My life revolved around our times together.

My wife, Sarah, and I went to see the movie *Secret Lives of Dentists*, a comedy showing at the local art house theatre. The plot had an uncanny resemblance to what was going on in my life at the time.

Two dentists are in practice together. The wife, trying to get a life outside of work and family, sings in the chorus of the local opera company. On opening night the whole family is there, and the husband goes backstage to give the wife a good-luck charm one of the kids forgot to give Mom. Mom is in the arms of another man, obviously in love. Believe it or not, it's a comedy, because the husband dentist starts having imaginary conversations with one of his difficult patients, played by the great comedian Denis Leary. The dentists patch things up. They stay in the marriage.

On the drive home, Sarah is completely mystified. "Why did the wife have the affair?" she asked.

"Because she needed to breathe," I answered.

Rendezvous in my office were nice, but we thought a trip together would be even better. I was to attend a four-day meeting on lung pathology in Orlando, Florida, which would last four days. I invited Annie to come along, and she said yes. Life is good, no?

The trip took place Thursday to Sunday in the first week in December. We would miss some Christmas parties, but that was okay. We would be together for four days.

We went to Pleasure Island, which was Magic Kingdom for grownups, with comedy clubs and shows with professional singers and dancers. We danced too, at a place that played Golden Oldies music. We were teenagers again.

But we did adult stuff also. On Friday night we had dinner at Victoria and Albert's, a restaurant where a jacket and a tie were required. I had the best-tasting meal I've ever had in my life, in a simple but elegant setting, with one musician on-site – a harp player. Pretty darn romantic.

I attended the medical course during the day, which unfortunately was pretty worthless. I signed up hoping to learn a workable approach to non-cancerous lung diseases – pattern recognition and nomenclature that I could use in my day-to-day practice of pathology, but that didn't happen. Instead, the course directors went on a tangent covering the manifestations of one disease – sarcoidosis – information not particularly useful to me.

During the day Annie studied also. She was taking courses at Middle Tennessee State University to get an MBA degree. So she studied business textbooks and worked on her projects. We spent the evenings and nights together.

The trip was a roller coaster. We were extraordinarily happy at times, and then for no reason Annie would start crying. When we were doing things – going out to eat, having fun at Pleasure Island, making love – we were happy. When we weren't doing things and had time to contemplate our future, which was bleak – we were sad.

So, Jack, how do you defend your adultery?

Of course I don't. I can't.

But here's the thing, how it can happen. I think we, all of us, are thrown into a tough world full of hardship, drudgery, boredom, competition, and violence. Certainly in many ways we live in a beautiful world, but in many ways it is also an uninviting world, even a dangerous one.

The Pacific, a miniseries, describes the experiences of marines in the South Pacific battles against Japan during World War II. As I watched the ten-part miniseries, I was struck by how life can be like the experiences of those marines. I know it's a horrible metaphor, but please cut me some slack here as I try to make a point. These marines, thrown into a horrible situation, did what they had to do to survive. It was kill the enemy or be killed. All the stuff they learned in Bible School and Western civilization classes – turn the other cheek, fair play, chivalry…well, that didn't apply on the battlefield.

I have not gone through anything remotely as tough as what those warriors went through, but…I'm just saying that as I watched the miniseries, it seemed to me to be a metaphor for some things that happen in life, as we live it. None of us chose to be born. We were thrown into this situation, this world, which in many ways is inhospitable. Life is hard, very hard. I've had to compete for everything I have, and at least for me, it's been a battle to survive. My perception is that I am surrounded by people just as smart, strong, and talented as I am, who want what I have – my job, my success, my everything – and the only way I can keep what I have is to work at least as hard as the competition, or harder. Am I unique in feeling this way? I doubt it.

Sooo…

If a talented, attractive, smart woman like Annie Layne comes into my life, who is interested in me, and the feeling is mutual, I am not going to say to myself: "Wait a minute, I can't do this, I'm married." Life is too short and too difficult to throw away a chance for joy. If that breaks some rules that I didn't write, that others did, well…

Of course, the rules of life are there for a reason, and you break them at your peril.

After we returned from Orlando, we continued the affair. As I write these words, it all seems so sordid, and it probably was, but it didn't seem that way at the time. We were in love.

Of course, like everyone who gets involved in the mess of an affair, there was no solution that left everyone happy. To turn this love triangle back to a straight narrow line needed an equation I couldn't come up with. The best solution to the problem would be to never get involved with somebody else in the first place, and stay in the marriage – but it was too late for that!

I got depressed.

Depression strikes when you're in a situation and you can't decide what to do, when there seems to be no solution, and the energy used up to find a solution that doesn't exist just drains you of all your feel-good hormones and chemicals. You feel like a rat in a maze, with no way out. Death looks like a reasonable alternative. I have no data, but I strongly suspect that many unexplained suicides, which apparently happen for "no apparent reason," are guys and gals trapped in an affair, who don't want the scandal of an affair and a divorce, but don't want to stay in a loveless marriage either. Faced with an insoluble problem, death seems like a solution.

So, dear readers, if you enter into an affair, know that you are starting a perilous journey, one you may not survive.

I was walking in a hospital hallway, on the way to do an operating room consult. A short distance ahead of me Dr. Tom Bruno, the orthopedic surgeon, and Annie were walking close together and talking. Neither one noticed me, only each other. Annie shined her *Mona Lisa* smile on Dr. Tom Bruno, showing extreme interest in every word he said. They got closer. Annie saw me. By that time I had reached the operating room suite, which I entered. I did my job, but I could scarcely breathe.

When I got back to my office, my phone rang, and I picked up. It was Annie.

"Are you interested in Dr. Bruno?" I asked.

"No," she said. "He means nothing to me."

"You seemed interested," I said.

"Look, I'm a single woman, on my own, and I do what I have to do to survive. If you are willing to make the commitment, I'll change. In the meantime, it's a tough world out there."

The movie *Body Heat* is about an affair. Mattie and her adulterous lover, Ned, contemplate murdering Mattie's husband. Ned is a lawyer and consults with one of his criminal clients about the best way to do that. His client tries to talk Ned out of it and says: "Anytime you try a decent crime, you got fifty ways to mess it up, and if you think of twenty-five of them, you're a genius, and you ain't no genius."

Similar reasoning applies to an affair. There are at least fifty ways to get caught, and if you think of twenty-five of them, you're a genius, and I'm no genius.

A couple of months after our Orlando trip, in early February, my boys and I came home from a Kentucky-Ivory basketball game. Sarah met us at the door and sent the boys upstairs. When we were alone, she asked, "Who is Annie Layne?"

"She's a co-worker," I mumbled. "You've met her. Why?"

Sarah pulled out a bunch of receipts with Annie's name on them, the evidence of the trip to Orlando Annie and I had taken together. To this day I don't know how Sarah got those receipts. How stupid!? But that didn't matter, I was caught.

I stammered out an explanation, which I don't think Sarah bought for a second. But it didn't make any difference. What was she looking for when she went through my papers that I should have been more careful to discard, or that Annie had passed on to her, or....who knows how she obtained them? I mean, what was Sarah looking for? She had to know what she would find, right?

What Sarah didn't know, what Annie didn't know, what I didn't know – was whether I was going to leave the marriage or not – one of the few times in life I have had total free will. I had to decide and decide fast.

Which I did. In fact, there was no indecision whatsoever. I stayed in the marriage. So did Sarah.

I broke up with Annie the next day. Annie was scheduled to be off that day, so she wasn't at the hospital, but she came to my office late that afternoon when everyone was gone. She wore a black jogging suit with red stripes down the sides. I was still dressed in my work clothes – maroon scrubs. Annie came in my office, closed the door, and kissed me in the usual fashion. Then she sat across the desk from me, ready to talk and share what had happened to each of us during the day, like we usually did.

"I want out," I said.

She didn't see it coming.

"At least for a while," I said.

Annie stood up, glared at me, close to tears. "It's over forever," she said. She walked out and slammed the door behind her.

I sat motionless, looking at the closed door.

A few minutes later Annie opened the door and sat down. She was crying and obviously had been crying since she left. "I'm not going to let you off that easy," she said. "Why?"

"You're sure you want to hear this?"

She nodded.

"You are a threat to my family."

"How?"

"My wife found out about us, never mind how. I don't want to leave the marriage, especially with a fourteen-year-old son at home. He will leave home when he's eighteen, but I don't want to lose these last four years with him."

"You don't have to miss those last four years with him. Just add me to your family."

For a beat I was speechless. Then I said, "The first time you came into contact with any of my sons, my wife would dynamite the both of us."

Annie sobbed convulsively. I had nothing to say. What could I say? That I wasn't worth it? That was and is certainly true, but I didn't think saying that would help.

After a few minutes she regained her composure. She said: "All these years I've turned down passes – sent these married guys back to their wives – I thought that's what single women should do with married guys who are interested in them. But eventually you get lonely enough, and ONE TIME I give in, and I'm the only one who gets hurt."

I said, "I don't think you really believe that."

Annie shook her head, took a deep breath, and for the last time, walked out. We never spoke again.

A few weeks later we both attended the monthly Surgery Department meeting. It was held in a large room, with long folding tables arranged in a rectangle. Annie and I arrived early, about fifteen minutes before the 7 a.m. meeting started. There were a handful of other early arrivals, so we weren't the only ones there. Annie sat directly across from me. The remaining members of the department straggled in, took their seats, and perused the paperwork. I glanced at the info and the agenda, and none of it concerned me, so I looked up at Annie. She was looking directly at me. It was like we were the only people in the room – no one else around, no sound, no commotion, nothing else – just the two of us looking at each other. She shined her *Mona Lisa* smile at me. We stared at each other for what seemed like a long time, but was probably just a minute or two. Then I looked away.

Two years later Annie married Tom Bruno, the orthopedic surgeon, who left his wife for Annie, something I was not willing to do. Annie left Excel McClain Hospital and went to work as Dr. Tom Bruno's office nurse and business manager. With her nursing education, MBA, and experience in the operating room, I'm sure Annie was a very able professional and personal assistant for Dr. Bruno. Lucky man.

A couple of years after that, Dr. Bruno retired, and so did Annie. For the next several years the only time I saw Annie, if I saw her at all, was at the annual Excel McClain Christmas party. Sometimes Sarah and I went to the party; sometimes we didn't. Same with Dr. Tom Bruno and Mrs. Annie Layne Bruno – sometimes they attended and sometimes not; if they came, they usually arrived early and left early. I never spoke to Annie, and she never spoke to me. We walked right past each other. What was there to say?

Twenty years after our affair began, Annie Layne Bruno died at age sixty-six of ovarian cancer. Her obituary in the *Siegeburg Post* described how "she was completely devoted to her husband and loved him with every ounce of her being."

A few days later I had a dream. I'm at a party, a dinner dance in a ballroom, and so is Annie. I'm standing at one side of the room, and Annie is standing across the room. We gaze at each other over the tables and seated guests. We are the only ones standing. A chamber orchestra starts playing dance music, not loud music, just nice music, background music. Dinner ends, the tables are cleared, and it's time for dancing. Annie and I are still looking at each other, across the room, across the music. Soon everyone is up and dancing – except Annie and I are not dancing. I stand and continue to look right at Annie, standing, and she looks right at me, the way she looked at me at Gretchen's Pizza, decades earlier. I am close enough to see that she is young, the way she was when I loved her, but I still love her, and I will love her until the end of time. We look at each other, ignoring the dancers, the orchestra, the servers, and partygoers – seeing only each other. She smiles at me one last time, shrugs, and walks away.

SELLOUT

June 2007

There were two hospitals in Siegeburg:

1. Excel McClain Hospital had been around the longest, essentially as long as the town itself. It was owned by Excel Corp, which owned a chain of 183 hospitals.
2. Healthcorp Hospital of Siegeburg was built five years ago. It was owned by Healthcorp Inc., which owned more hospitals than Excel Corp. It owned more hospitals than anybody in the world.

Both hospitals were about the same size, around 220 beds. They competed for patients and the associated revenues. It was war, complete with an arms race – who had the best MRI machine, CT scanner, endoscopy equipment... as well as competition for the best standing army, i.e., the best doctors and nurses. The citizens of Siegeburg thought having two hospitals was good – the competition made both places better, so that they provided good medical care and service to the community. Those who actually worked at the two hospitals thought differently, that cooperation and working together would result in better patient care.

On a Monday afternoon, two men in suits sat, drank coffee, and talked. The setting was the boardroom of Excel McClain Hospital. A large oval oak table occupied most of the rectangular room. The wall opposite the single entrance had a counter about waist high, with coffee apparatus dominating the far corner. The wall above the counter had built-in bookshelves, which were filled with binders containing documents – bylaws, minutes of meetings, plans, and other excreta of the hospital bureaucracy. The wall to the right of the entrance was replaced by floor-to-ceiling windows so one could look out and see the entrance to the hospital covered by a green awning and past that a vista of parking lots for visitors and patients. The green window curtains were closed, so the overhead fluorescent lights were the only illumination. Framed certificates from various accrediting and regulating authorities covered the remaining two walls. A portable white screen was set up on the floor near one end of the table, opposite the window, and it faced a computer and projector on one end of the table. The projector was still warm after the just concluded Medical Executive Committee meeting. The PowerPoint presentation with statistics of hospital admissions, surgical case numbers, emergency room visits, revenues, and other "monitors" had clicked and clicked until everyone was dizzy and sleepy. When the meeting adjourned, the physicians left rapidly.

The two men in suits, who were not physicians, stayed behind.

One was Peter White. He was a roly-poly bear of a man, with dark hair combed straight back, leaving a V in front. His most noticeable feature was a perpetual smart-ass grin. He was in his mid-fifties. He was the southeast regional vice president of Excel Corp and a very rich man.

The other man was Bryan Magnuson, who was short and slim, with the appearance of a long-distance runner, which he was. His hair was sandy and cut short. The light brown hair of his mustache and goatee was longer than the hair at the top of his head. He was in his early fifties. He was CEO of Excel McClain Hospital and wanted to be a very rich man.

Peter was Bryan's boss.

"So are you on board with this stuff?" asked Peter.

"I don't know. I guess."

One of the ladies from the kitchen staff came in to clear the table of coffee cups, saucers, napkins, and the other detritus of the meeting. She moved the contents of the table onto her cart. She wore white – white scrubs, white apron, and a white cap covering her hair. The two men ignored her.

"Ever notice how all medical staffs are the same?" asked Peter.

"No. I haven't really thought about it," said Bryan.

"You don't get around as much as I do," said Peter. "You will. Keep your eyes open. Observe."

"Observe what?" asked Bryan.

"Every medical staff has a crusty ole doc, an old surgeon, general practitioner, whatever – who has been around forever – older than dirt. He perceives himself to be the patriarch of medicine, but hell, he's not even board certified. He barely has a medical license! All his hospital privileges were grandfathered in, so he's exempt from proving that he's qualified to do anything, so he doesn't know what he's doing and kills patients right and left. But here's the crazy thing: his patients love him – 'good ole doc' they say 'practices good old-fashioned medicine,' which unfortunately is ineffective or worse. No one in authority does anything about the situation, because 'good ole doc' brings patients to the hospital and referrals to other physicians."

Bryan said, "That would be Dr. Bob McClain, good old Dr. Bob. He's not around anymore, but he was a real big shot – hell, the hospital is named after him, well, his father actually, but I see your point."

"Of course you do. Then there's the idealist, who comes out of med school and residency and wants to save the world. He thinks being a doctor is a calling, like the ministry or something, and God sent him to save everybody."

"You are talking about our internist, Steve Prescott. Always wants to change everything, almost single-handedly caused Dr. Bob to retire, which probably needed to happen, but still, what a pain!"

Peter nodded in agreement. He said, "Then you have a middle-aged guy, usually a surgeon, who is as jaded as the idealist is innocent. He's been around long enough to know that you can't change anything. He's tried, tried hard, to make things better, but all he has to show for his efforts is a bunch of mental scar tissue. He's as cynical as a veteran of the Peace Corps and just grumbles and goes along to get along."

"That would be Mitch Thornburg, our surgeon, who brings about a million dollars of patient revenue to the hospital each month, what with all the operations he does. But he's burnt out. I think he will be retiring as soon as he can."

"You're a bright guy. You're getting the hang of it. Then you have a physician, always suspicious, thinks that everyone is out to get him, but he's wrong, no one even cares about him. He's the only one who thinks he's important. To everyone else he's a nobody. It's kind of funny, really."

"Morris Benson, our gastroenterologist," said Bryan.

The lady from the kitchen staff finished clearing the table, rolled the cart to the door, and opened it. She was a little overweight and moved slowly out of the room. Neither man helped her. She closed the door as she exited.

Peter continued, "Right, the guy asking me all the questions about whether this hospital was going to be sold or not. Dr. Benson thinks he's a really smart savvy guy, since he's been to med school and all, but he don't know shit."

"Actually, that was a good question," said Bryan.

"Yeah, but for the wrong reasons. This sale has nothing to do with him. Dr. Benson is barely a pawn in this chess game, but we'll get back to that."

"Okay."

"Then there's the motherly type, usually a pediatrician, who doesn't have the business sense to run a bake sale, let alone a medical practice, and meet a payroll. Therefore she runs her practice at break-even or worse. Since she doesn't make any money, she can't hire anyone to join her practice and help out, so she works all the time and has no life – and still doesn't make any money."

"That would be Dr. Diane Murtaugh, who used to work here. She had some issues and had to move away."

"And finally we have the hospital-based physicians – the radiologists, anesthesiologists, pathologists, and ER docs – the RAPERS if you will. The less said about those bottom feeders, the better. They are clowns, pretending to be real doctors caring about patients, when all they really care about is money."

"As opposed to real doctors who don't care about money?" said Bryan.

"Right." Peter laughed.

"As opposed to us," said Bryan. "What do we care about other than money?"

Peter said, "Not a damn thing. That's the spirit!"

The door opened, and Richard from maintenance/information technology checked out the computer and projector and powered everything down. He folded up the screen and walked out of the room with it. He was a muscular, athletic-looking guy with broad shoulders and made it look easy. As Richard left, Bryan thanked him.

There was silence for a beat. Then Peter said, "So are you on board with this stuff?"

"Well, I'm not happy about it," said Bryan.

"I'm not asking you to be happy about it. I just want you to be comfortable about it. We can't do this without you."

"I'm not real good at dissembling."

"Who is? Look, I'm not asking you to lie. I'm not asking you to betray your country or anything. I mean, no one is going to die when this hospital is sold. In fact, patients will live. It's a good thing. You'll be helping people, and you sure as hell will be helping yourself."

"So when someone asks me if McClain hospital is going to be sold, and someone will ask, I'm supposed to say Excel McClain Hospital is not for sale?"

"Absolutely."

"My credibility will be shot."

"Who cares?"

"I care."

"So tell them some garbage – something along the lines that you don't know what is going to happen."

Bryan shrugged, unconvinced.

Peter continued, "Or blame it all on me. Tell everyone that I told you that the hospital was not for sale."

"That's just another lie, doesn't really help me."

Peter said, "Look, when Healthcorp buys this hospital, you will be taken care of."

"How?"

"When this deal closes, you will get a two-hundred-thousand-dollar bonus, a token of appreciation from Excel."

"I appreciate that."

"And you will have the option of going to work for Healthcorp, maybe even staying here, going to work at their Siegeburg Hospital."

"I dunno. They have always been the competition. I don't know how I would feel going to work over there."

"Well, Excel and Healthcorp are going to need your help with the transition after the sale."

"I can do that."

Peter said, "Then, if you don't want to work for Healthcorp, you can continue to work for us. Heck, you can continue to work for me if you want. We work well together. You will probably have to move, but we can arrange a position for you somewhere, probably a promotion. See, you have all kinds of options. This event can be a great career move for you. All you have to do is keep your mouth shut."

"Right. But I'm not sure what you even need me for."

"You're too smart to ask such a question. Look, we had a similar situation up in Kentucky. We had a hospital about this size competing with another hospital in town – a Healthcorp hospital, about the same size as us. Like here, the Kentucky town wasn't big enough to support two hospitals. And like here, the Healthcorp hospital had a little bit of an edge – it was a little newer, a little bigger…let's face it – it was a better hospital."

"Same as here," said Bryan.

"Right," said Peter. "So patients and doctors started to gravitate to the competition, not enough at first to make much difference, but it was a trend in the wrong direction. We decided to sell our hospital, take our money, and get out."

"Same as here," said Bryan.

"But *unfortunately* rumors started that our hospital was going to close, and we weren't smart enough to push back hard. So there was a rush of doctors getting staff privileges at the other hospital and taking their patients there. Oh, and the patients – *they* wanted to go to the Healthcorp Hospital, because ours was 'fixin' to close.' Our volumes went down, way down. Then our staff started to worry about their future – wondered what would happen to them if the Excel Hospital closed. So our nurses, especially the good ones, and other hospital employees – *they* went to work at the Healthcorp. They wanted to go where they had a future."

Bryan shook his head. "Sounds like a mess."

Peter nodded, raised his eyebrows, and continued: "It was a disaster. Then it turned into a nightmare. Healthcorp decided *not* to buy the hospital, backed out of the deal. Their CEO told us 'why should we buy the hospital when we can get all their patients and doctors for nothing?'"

Peter paused and then continued, "Which is exactly what happened. Eventually we had so few patients and doctors that we had to close our hospital. We lost everything to Healthcare Corp, who gained 100% market share in that Kentucky town *without paying us one red cent.*"

Bryan said, "Yeah, I remember hearing something about that. I never heard the details."

"Well, now you have, and we can't let something like that happen here. This deal has to stay secret until it closes – got to – so help me God. We can't take another hit like that, closing a hospital and not getting anything for it."

Their coffee cups were empty; time to wrap things up.

"So what's the schedule?" asked Bryan.

"The people from Healthcorp will come here – go over the numbers, contracts, inventory, and a bunch of other crap – do their 'due diligence.' They aren't going to find out anything they don't already know, but it's got to be done. While that's going on, you need to keep your mouth shut about the hospital being sold. If anyone asks what's going on, you just mumble something about this being a routine audit – that this hospital is open for patients and doctors and will stay that way, and that you have no plans to leave Siegeburg, and neither does Excel Corp."

"Then what?"

"Then the deal is closed, we sell the hospital, make the announcement, and leave. Everyone is happy."

"Well, not everyone. Those who listen to me, believe me, and keep working here, keep taking care of patients – they'll lose their jobs when the hospital is closed."

Peter fixed himself another cup of coffee. So did Bryan.

Peter said, "Maybe you should prepare three letters."

"Huh," said Bryan.

"I guess you haven't heard that joke. It goes like this: A young man straight out of school takes over as CEO of a hospital from a grizzled veteran. The ambitious young man, eager to learn, asks if the older man has any advice to give. The exiting CEO gives the new CEO three sealed envelopes labeled on the outside **one**, **two**, and **three**, and says, 'Everything I know is in these three letters. If and when you get into trouble and don't see a way out, open one of these letters, in order, and do what it says.'

Things go okay at the hospital for about six months, but then problems come up – the nurses aren't happy, there are patient complaints, the physicians are rebellious, and there are just too many problems for the young CEO to solve. He opens the first envelope. It says:

"***Blame the prior administration.***

"Which doesn't make a whole lot of sense, but that's what the young CEO does. At every committee meeting, in his newsletter, and in private communications, his mantra is that all the problems of the hospital are the fault of the prior administration.

"Amazingly it works.

"A year goes by, and a different set of problems arises: the hospital does poorly on some inspections, there are regulatory issues, morale at the hospital is low, there's labor unrest, talk of forming a union…everything is going wrong, and every day there is a new crisis. He opens the second letter. It says:

"***Blame the medical staff.***

"The young CEO proceeds to blame all the problems on the medical staff, which solves everything. These letters are invaluable! The medical staff isn't too happy about what happens, but everyone else is. Things get back to normal, and the good times return.

"But of course the good times don't last. The local economy goes into a downturn, people lose their jobs and their health insurance, so hospital admissions go down, and revenue goes down. Once again the young man has problems he cannot solve. He opens the third letter. It says

"***Prepare three letters.***"

Bryan laughed.

"Prepare three letters," said Peter.

Peter hit the road. Bryan returned to his office, right next to the boardroom. His office also had windows looking out at the entrance and parking lot. Bryan liked to watch the patients and visitors come and go, liked the feeling that he was helping them, making a difference. Bryan looked out the windows for a while and pondered what to do.

He was going to have to lie. For the last five years, ever since the Siegeburg Healthcorp Hospital was built, Bryan had been forced to put down rumors that his hospital would be sold or closed down. Now that was really going to happen. And he couldn't confide in anybody. His friend, Kathy Lassiter, had been gone a couple of years – she'd gone over to the competition and moved to Arizona, where she was CEO of a Healthcorp Hospital. Bryan thought that it was not a good idea to phone her, an executive from the other side of the deal, and chat about what was going on. And he couldn't talk to his wife about the sale; he couldn't talk to his wife about much of anything.

Bryan decided to stop thinking about it, and settled in to do some work – review and sign minutes of various committee meetings, go over budgets, approve payment of invoices, worry…things he did every day.

Jack Spenser, the pathologist, knocked on his office door and came in. Bryan wasn't sure he had any friends at the hospital. If he had one, that would be Dr. Spenser.

Jack didn't sit down. "You didn't say much at the Executive Committee meeting. Anything going on?"

"Nope. Not a darn thing."

"Anything I should know about?"

"Nope."

"Why was Peter White here?"

"Just a routine visit, looking over the facility, checking out our numbers."

"It's been a while since he's come to an Executive Committee meeting."

"I think Peter just wanted to check in with you guys, see what's going on."

"He didn't say much."

"Things are quiet – not much to say."

Jack nodded and left.

A couple of days later it was bonus time. It was a good year for Excel Corp and a good year for Bryan. As promised, he received a bonus check of $200,000.00 – all that money, thought Bryan, just to keep his mouth shut.

There was a part of Bryan that wanted him to tell Peter and Excel to take their money and shove it. He wanted to be able to tell the truth to Jack and the other people who were going to lose their jobs when the hospital was sold. But he just couldn't do it. He just didn't have enough money. See, that's where the world gets you. It's nice to talk about integrity, honor, and telling the truth – if you're rich and "set," but that's a lot harder to do when you have to support yourself, as well as a family – sure is easier to keep quiet, feign ignorance, and go along.

And Bryan asked himself: Who is going to be hurt if I keep this secret? Sure, some people were going to lose their jobs when Excel McClain Hospital closed, but they were going to lose their jobs anyway. It was just a matter of timing – find out now or a few weeks later – in the meantime they would be taking care of patients who needed help. And even if Bryan told the truth, Excel would just send someone to replace him, and deny what Bryan said, someone like Peter White, or Peter White himself.

And it was even more complicated than that. Sure, Bryan has loyalty to Jack and the employees at Excel McClain Hospital, and owed it to them to tell them the truth so that they could make plans for their future. But Bryan also had loyalty to Peter White and Excel Corp. They had trusted Bryan with the responsibility for the hospital. The company had been loyal to him. Not only that, but Excel paid Bryan's salary, the money that put a roof over his family's head, put food on the table, and paid for private education for his boys. What was that worth? It was worth a lot!

What do you do, when one standard, telling the truth, contradicts another standard, loyalty to an employer?

Bryan decided to do what he was told, keep quiet, and cash the bonus. That way Bryan could prove that he was a team player, and hopefully get promoted to bigger and better positions with Excel Corp. He had a bright future. Maybe Bryan would be CEO of Excel Corp someday! Stranger things have happened.

So Bryan lied to anyone who asked if the hospital was going to be sold. And a little bit of Bryan's soul died.

Friday, four weeks later

The front page of the *Siegeburg Post* trumpeted the news with this headline on the front page: "HEALTHCARE CORPORATION PURCHASES MCCLAIN HOSPITAL FROM EXCEL CORPORATION."

The article had a question-answer section between the paper and the CEO of the Siegeburg Healthcorp Hospital, John Jones:

Post: Please briefly explain the terms of the purchase.

Jones: Simply put, this is an acquisition, not a merger.

Post: What will happen to the McClain Hospital facility?

Jones: No plans have been made. However, I can say that the healthcare needs of the Siegeburg community will be met by the Siegeburg Healthcorp Hospital.

Post: What will happen to the employees of Excel McClain Hospital?

Jones: I know that there are some talented people at the McClain facility, who are welcome to apply for jobs with us.

The paper did not interview Bryan Magnuson or anyone else from Excel McClain Hospital. No one wanted to read about the losers.

It was a great day for the Siegeburg Healthcorp Hospital people, and a sad day for those who loved Excel McClain Hospital, who got the news that they were out of a job from the newspaper.

Bryan Magnuson was busy. There was a steady stream of employees (nurses, technologists, clerical workers…) going in and out of Bryan's office all day. The conversations were all the same:

Employee: What does this mean for me?

Bryan: Your job here is ending.

Employee: Will I get a job at the Healthcorp Hospital?

Bryan: You can apply. I don't know how many people they will hire. I don't work there.

Employee: Will I get severance pay?

Bryan: Yes, two weeks.

Employee: What about health insurance?

Bryan: You can sign up for COBRA.

Employee: Isn't that expensive?

Bryan: I think it is.

Employee: Did you know this was going to happen?

Bryan: No.

Absolutely no one believed that last part.

Most of the physicians at Excel McClain Hospital weren't affected much. Instead of admitting their patients to Excel McClain Hospital, they would start admitting their patients to the Siegeburg Healthcorp Hospital – no big deal. The internists, surgeons, obstetricians-gynecologists, pediatricians and other clinicians would still have patients and still have jobs. Therefore it was easy for them to go around the Excel McClain Hospital, comforting the employees. For example, Mitch Thornberg and Rob Masterson went to the operating room suite break room, sat down, and tried to reassure the OR nurses that everything would be alright. Easy for them to say. The OR nurses cried anyway.

So did the laboratory staff. Dr. Jack Spenser walked around the lab, trying to console the technologists and other workers in the lab. Some of them would get jobs at the Siegeburg Healthcorp hospital, because there was a shortage of lab workers. Dr. Spenser would not get a job at the other hospital. There was not a shortage of pathologists.

At the end of the day Jack Spenser went to Bryan's office.

"Did you know?" asked Jack.

"No," said Bryan. "I was as surprised as everybody else."

Jack didn't say anything, just nodded his head, and walked out. They never spoke again.

Bryan didn't do much talking to anyone after that day. Excel prepared a memo/letter to the Excel McClain Hospital employees, which answered most of the questions the employees had directed to Bryan. Two weeks later he moved to Florida, where he became CEO of a 334-bed hospital, which was a little larger than Excel McClain Hospital. It was a promotion. His compensation went up. He was a team player.

And he knew what it meant to sell out.

Epilogue

Present Day

At the corner of Cambridge and Autumn Streets, the abandoned McClain Hospital is guarded by a high fence with razor wire on top, so you can't get close to it. Probably just as well. It's not a pretty sight, because it's been vacant for many years. The building is surprisingly solid, but the windows and doors are missing, and the interior has been vandalized. It's hard to believe that for almost a century it was a place of hope for those who needed medical care. For over a quarter of a century I worked as a pathologist there. It was my life.

When Excel McClain Hospital closed, I was out of a job. The Siegeburg Healthcorp Hospital did not need another pathologist. Maybe I could have gotten a job somewhere else, maybe not. At any rate, I didn't feel like moving. Siegeburg is my home. I will be buried here.

So I stopped practicing medicine and did what Dr. Callister suggested I do, decades earlier: write stories, the stories that I could tell, the stories that only I could tell.

This is my third book, with more to come. I will be writing until the day I die.

Jack Spenser, M.D.

GLOSSARY

AOA: Stands for Alpha Omega Alpha, an honor society for medical students. I was not a member, so I don't know much about it. I have noticed, though, that being in AOA seems to be an adverse prognostic indicator for how well that medical student would do later in real medical practice. That is to say, my observation is that, for the most part, AOA members have tended to have mediocre careers, or worse. The students in my class who went on to have stellar careers (e.g., joined the medical school faculty at Harvard, established a medical media company worth billions) were *not* members of AOA. In fact, they almost flunked out.

Ambu bag: Hooks up to an intubation tube that has been inserted into a patient's trachea. The ambu bag can be compressed by hand to move air in and out of the patient's lungs.

Antecubital: Front of the elbow, where it bends.

Antecubital vein: Blood vessel in the bend of the elbow, a common place to draw blood.

Asystole: Heart with no activity at all.

Atrial Flutter: Abnormal heart rhythm. The goal of a cardiologist is to convert that to a normal rhythm — "normal sinus rhythm."

Baseline: The status of the patient at the start, before a treatment or therapeutic maneuver.

Bilirubin: A chemical that results from the breakdown of red blood cells. It's yellow, so excess bilirubin causes jaundice.

Biopsy: A small tissue sample.

Bone marrow biopsy: Small sample of bone and bone marrow, which can be processed into slides to look at with a microscope.

Cachectic: A wasted appearance, like that seen in concentration camp survivors.

Celiac disease: A disease caused by a reaction to eating gluten, which is found in foods derived from wheat and other grains.

Clot section: Bone marrow that clots and can be processed, just like tissue, into microscopic slides to look at under a microscope.

Colonic polyps: Growths in the colon or rectum. Most polyps are benign, but many are premalignant. A few are malignant. When a gastroenterologist sees one during a colonoscopy, he or she will try to remove it, or at least sample it, and send it to the pathologist for examination.

Colonoscope/colonoscopy: A viewing lens is attached to the end of a long flexible tube, which is threaded into the anus to reach as far as the small intestine, but no further.

CT: Abbreviation for CAT SCAN, a fancy complicated X-ray study that gives a really good picture of the anatomy of the part of the body studied and any abnormalities.

Cytogenetics: Study of cells in terms of chromosome/DNA makeup. Because malignant cells (e.g., leukemia, malignant lymphoma…) tend to have chromosome/DNA abnormalities, studying the cytogenetics of a patient's malignant tumor cells can be helpful in terms of diagnosis and treatment.

Duodenum: Part of the small bowel, just past the stomach.

Endoscopy procedures: Using a lens at the end of a flexible tube to look at a patient's anatomy – rectum, colon, esophagus, stomach, duodenum…

Endothelium: Inner lining of a blood vessel.

Endotracheal tube: Tube that goes from the opening of the mouth to the trachea, used to transport air/oxygen to a patient unable to breathe without assistance.

Eosin: A dye used along with another stain (hematoxylin) to stain tissue sections so a pathologist can see things with a microscope and make diagnoses. The eosin makes the tissue show up red. The hematoxylin makes the tissue show up blue. No one knows why the stains react with tissues the way they do, to make such diagnostic beauty. It's witchcraft.

Esophago/gastro/duodenoscopy: A viewing lens is attached to the end of a long flexible tube, which can be threaded into the mouth to reach the esophagus, stomach, and duodenum.

Esophagus: Tube that goes from the pharynx to the stomach.

Etiology: Cause of.

Flow cytometry: A specialty study that involves sending an emulsion ("flow") through an instrument that analyses one cell at a time, either by chemical reaction or light pattern, or both, to discern what type of cell it is ("cytometry"). It sounds complicated, and it is, and I don't really understand it. That's the best I can do.

Gastroenterologist: Internal medicine specialist in stomach and intestinal disorders, as well as liver diseases.

Grandfathered in: When criteria for what a physician is qualified to do are changed, **but** the changes do not apply to those already on the medical staff when the changes are made – how nice for them.

Hemosiderosis: Derived from the word hemosiderin, a breakdown product of red blood cell destruction, with resultant iron deposits.

Heparin: A drug that prevents blood from clotting.

Hereditary spherocytosis: A hereditary disease associated with abnormal red blood cells. The red blood cells are small and have a spherical shape rather than the shape of biconcave discs. The patients affected with this disorder have dysfunctional red blood cells.

HIV antibody test: Another one of those tests I don't really understand. It's a test that is positive in patients with HIV/AIDS infection. It can also be positive for other reasons though ("false positives"), so a positive HIV antibody test has to be "confirmed" by a Western blot test – another test I don't understand.

Hematologist: Physician who treats diseases of the blood – anemia, leukemia, lymphoma and the like.

Hematoxylin: See definition for eosin.

Histotechnologist: A person who makes the microscopic slides for a pathologist to look at. To write the histotechnologist's job description would take a book longer than the one you are reading. Briefly, it requires knowledge and skill to use a tissue processor (to process the tissue), paraffin dispenser (to make paraffin blocks), a microtome (with a sharp knife to cut thin slices of tissue from the paraffin blocks and put them on glass slides), and staining techniques (to stain the slides). Most of this cannot be taught. A person either has the knack for doing histotechnology or not. What histotechnologists do is witchcraft.

Ichthyologist: Scientist who studies fish.

Idiopathic: Of unknown cause – very commonly used when it comes to medicine.

Idiopathic Thrombocytopenic Purpura: Low platelet count for unknown reasons. It is a diagnosis made after other diseases have been excluded.

Iliac Crest: Top part of that large bone in the hip region – a bulwark.

Intubation kit: Has the equipment used to establish an air source for someone who can't breathe. It includes a scope for looking down the patient's larynx, to see what you're doing, and a tube to place down a patient's mouth and insert into the trachea. That tube can then be hooked up to air or oxygen, whatever is needed.

Investigational Review Board (IRB): A committee of an institution that ensures any research done by the institution is ethical.

Kaposi's sarcoma: A malignant tumor of blood vessels, seen in old patients only, until the AIDS epidemic, when it became one of the hallmarks of the disease.

Labs: Medical slang for laboratory results.

Laryngoscope: A relatively short tube with a lens at the end, which is used to go into the mouth, down the throat, and to the larynx. It is used by anesthesiologists and those doing cardiopulmonary resuscitation to visualize and guide a tube (intubation tube) through the larynx into the trachea. The end of the tube opposite the trachea is hooked up to air/oxygen for the patient to breathe.

Macrophages: White blood cells that eat stuff.

Manichean: Belief that the affairs of the world and the universe are best understood as perpetual conflict between intrinsic good and intrinsic evil.

Meningococcemia: Meningococcus bacteria in the bloodstream, very often fatal.

Morphology: How things look.

MRI: An X-ray study, using magnetic resonance imaging, whatever that is!? At any rate, the important thing to know is that the resulting images are of high quality, revealing anatomy and abnormalities of the part of the body examined. It sure beats having to do surgery to "explore" the region and see what's wrong.

Myelodysplastic syndrome (MDS): A poorly understood disease, in which the bone marrow does not make red blood cells, white blood cells, and platelets the way it is supposed to, so the patient suffers from anemia, low white blood cell counts, and low platelet counts. The normal cells of the bone marrow are replaced by poorly formed cells, bizarre looking, that do not function and do not become functional red blood cells, white blood cells or platelets. Sometimes the disease turns into leukemia.

Usually the cause of MDS is unknown, and we don't know much about the disease. That's why this definition is longer than any other definition in this glossary. The less I know about a subject, the longer the explanation. When I write surgical pathology reports, the length of the report about a specimen correlates inversely with my knowledge of it: the short reports are definitive and helpful to the clinicians – the long reports are rambling discussions, useless, kind of like this definition.

National Practitioner Data Bank: A database filled with the misdeeds of miscreant physicians – malpractice judgments and settlements, actions hospitals or licensing boards take against physicians…It is maintained by the government. Remember the expression in school "This goes on your *permanent record.*" That's what the Data Bank is.

Neuroanatomy: Anatomy of the brain and spinal cord.

Neuropathy: Nerve pain, which tends to affect the nerves at the periphery of the body, e.g., hands and feet.

Nomenclature: How things are named and classified.

Non-compete clause: A clause commonly used in the employment agreement when a new physician joins the practice of an established physician. It basically says that the new physician can't come in, grab the established physician's patients, and then move next door (or close by), taking those patients with him or her. It has never been clear to me if these non-compete clauses are enforceable or not.

Oncologist: An internist who treats cancer. Of course this can involve chemotherapy, which can kill you, radiation, which can kill you, and radical surgery, which can kill you. To summarize, an oncologist is a doctor who *hates* cancer more than he loves patients.

Osmotic fragility test: One of those blood tests that I don't really understand, but goes something like this: Red blood cells are subjected to various solutions that make them swell up. If the red blood cells are abnormal in size or shape (e.g., hereditary spherocytosis), they will be "fragile," and the test detects that. If a person's red blood cells are normal, the test will be normal.

Pathophysiology: The processes that lead to a disease.

Platelets: Little particles in the blood, made by the bone marrow, that are indispensable in preventing bleeding that would kill you.

Pharmacology: Study of drugs.

Pharynx: Short tube that goes from the mouth to the esophagus (it's at the back of the throat).

Phlebotomist: A technician from the lab who draws blood from patients.

Platelets: Little particles in the blood that help blood clot when needed.

Portacaval shunt: An operation in which a connection is made between the portal vein ("porta") and inferior vena cava ("caval"). These are two huge blood vessels (veins) located around the liver. The purpose of the operation is to relieve high pressure in the portal vein, which can be caused by a damaged liver and be life threatening.

Propofol: Medicine an anesthesiologist uses to induce loss of consciousness during an operation (e.g., bone marrow procedure).

PTT: Stands for Partial Thromboplastin Time – forget that – the only thing you need to know for the purpose of this book is that it is a blood test that uses clotting to monitor heparin drug levels, to make sure the dosage is correct.

Pulmonary: Having to do with the lungs.

Pulmonologist: Lung specialist.

Respiratory: Having to do with breathing.

Sarcoidosis: Yet another disease we don't understand. Its hallmark is a pattern of inflammation ("granuloma") that is typical of tuberculosis or fungus infections, but can be seen secondary to countless other diseases. The diagnosis of sarcoidosis is made this way: We investigate all the possible causes for granulomas, and if we do not find a cause, we call the disease sarcoidosis.

Scut work: Work done to help patients that is a nuisance, that nobody wants to do, but has to be done, usually by medical students, interns, and residents with little power. Examples of scut work are drawing blood, starting intravenous lines, giving an enema, putting in urinary catheters, placing nasogastric tubes in a patient's nose and guiding it to the stomach, and various simple lab tasks (urinalysis, making peripheral blood smears and the like).

Serology: Study a disease by the reaction of the body to that disease – detecting the proteins (antibodies) that respond to fight an infection or other cause of inflammation.

Spherocytosis: Abnormal red blood cells, shaped as spheres rather than biconcave discs, so they do not function normally.

Sternum: Breast bone at the front of the chest.

Thrombotic Thrombocytopenic Purpura: A blood disorder associated with blood clots, which leads to decreased platelets and bleeding. The disorder also causes anemia because of the bleeding, as well as mechanical breakdown of red blood cells that are damaged by the clots. It is a very serious life-threatening disease.

Trachea: Anatomical structure, a tube that goes from the larynx to the lungs.

Xylocaine: Medicine used to make a local part of the body numb, so the patient feels no pain during a procedure, e.g., bone marrow procedure.

Vasculitis: Inflammation of the blood vessels. White blood cells infiltrate the structures of the vessel walls, with deleterious consequences like swelling, bleeding, and loss of function.

Ventricular fibrillation: Abnormal heart rhythm in which the heart beats irregularly and ineffectively.

Ventricular tachycardia: Abnormal heart rhythm resulting in a fast heart rate. Goal of a cardiologist is to convert this abnormal rhythm to a normal one – "normal sinus rhythm."

Western Blot Test: A lab test which can be used to "confirm" an HIV antibody test. If the HIV antibody test is positive **and** the patient has various risk factors for HIV infection **and** a positive Western blot test – the patient probably has an HIV/AIDS infection.

ABOUT THE AUTHOR

Dr. Spenser is a practicing physician who has written several scientific articles in various medical journals. This is his third book.

ALSO BY JACK SPENSER, M.D.

Diary of a Malpractice Lawsuit:
A Physician's Journey and Survival Guide

You Can't not Know: A Memoir about Medical School,
Residency, and Life